The Disappearance of Jim Sullivan

Tanguy Viel

THE DISAPPEARANCE OF JIM SULLIVAN

Translated from the French by Clayton McKee

DALKEY ARCHIVE PRESS
Dallas / Dublin

Originally published in Éditions de Minuit as *La Disparition de Jim Sullivan* in 2013.

First Dalkey Archive edition, 2021.

ISBN: 9781628973716
CIP data available on request.

www.dalkeyarchive.com
Dallas / Dublin

Printed on permanent/durable acid-free paper.

Part I

Chapter 1

RECENTLY THINKING BACK over the books I'd read over the last few years, I noticed that there were more American novels than French novels on my bookshelves. For a long time, however, I still preferred to read French literature and to write books set in France with French stories and French characters. But it's true that over the last few years, I ended up telling myself that I'd reached some kind of terminus; that after all, my stories should take place somewhere else, in America, for example, in a shack by the edge of a large lake or a motel on Route 75—or anywhere really, so long as things got moving.

I think I gave up on France mainly because I found it too static, too petrified, somehow. At any rate, it didn't meet the need for air that I felt so intensely at that point in my life. It was a breath of fresh air when I read American novels—international novels, as I took to saying—which have been translated into every language and are sold in almost every bookstore.

I'm not saying that every international novel is an American novel; all I'm saying is that the main character in an international novel would never live in the shadow of Chartres Cathedral. Nor am I saying that I thought about placing a character in that city—although it must be said that there is the inconvenience that pretty much every French town has its cathedral and surrounding cobbled streets, which destroy the place's international dimension and make it hard for them to rise to any human universality. In this regard, Americans have a disturbing advantage over us: even when they set the action in Kentucky, among chicken farms and corn fields, they manage to make a novel international.

Even Montana. Even authors from Montana who write about hunting and fishing and gathering firewood for the winter write novels that sell just as many copies in Paris as in New York. I can't wrap my head around it. We have hectares of forests and rivers, we have a country that has twice the fishing and hunting of Montana, yet we can't manage to write international novels.

The day that I realized this—I must confess—I bought a map of America, hung it on the wall in my office, and said to myself that the entire story of my next book would be set there, in the United States.

It didn't take me long to choose the specific

region that would serve as the backdrop for my book: Detroit, Michigan, which is a truly international city. It's a city full of asphalt and rusty metal, a city of skyscrapers, endless avenues, and all the things you find in any other American city, like New York, or, as it happens, Detroit, which is just as modern as New York and Los Angeles, and in any case just as rich, from the novelistic point of view—although much poorer in actuality, now that it's in industrial decline. In any case, I believed it was the perfect city in which to set my novel.

For example, in Detroit—according to what I read on the Internet—you have 3,200 windows within your field of vision. I never fully understood what that meant, 3,200 windows at the same time; but I told myself that if I included something like that in my novel, readers would then be able to understand that my characters live in a big, complex, international city, a city full of glassy surfaces and promises. Likewise, I told myself that they would be able to get to know Dwayne Koster's ex-wife, because I've noticed that in American novels the main character is typically divorced. At least it's often at such a moment that the characters are revealed to us, around the age of fifty, when their personal life has become a bit complicated.

It's true that Dwayne Koster was exactly fifty when my story began, that his personal life had become slightly complicated, and that he was divorced, so that generally speaking there was no question of my departing from the main principles that have proven effective in American novels.

Chapter 2

DETROIT, 1805, I wrote: a gigantic fire razed the city, reducing it to a heap of ashes scattered over the ground; yet it was destined to be reborn from said ashes, just like the city's motto states: *Speramus meliora; resurget cineribus.*

There's no doubt that the enthusiastic pastor who proclaimed those words on that day in 1805 was not only unaware that they would be slapped across the façade of City Hall, but also that they would be so fitting two hundred years later, by which time Detroit had become one of the poorest cities in the United States, one of the most dangerous—I've also read—and one of the most depopulated, at least when it comes to the large neighborhoods that have been hastily vacated, abandoned to rust, broken glass, and the hundreds of stray dogs that roam the cold, dead factories, dropping dead in the snow before the end of winter.

It must be said that after a certain Cadillac planted his flag on Griswold Street in 1701, after a certain Pontiac tried to take over the city in 1763, and after a certain Ford set up shop in 1896, Detroit experienced the prophetic times foretold by the pastor and heralded by the new smoke of the automobiles. But the city seems in part to have returned to the ashes that haunted its birth, at least wherever abandonment allows the same dereliction to become manifest, which you can see in thousands of photos in circulation on the Internet: a wrecked piano in a dusty room, a rusty shopping cart in a mall, an edition of the *Times* in a devastated bedroom, a crystal chandelier smashed on the floor, a hospital bed buried under rubble. In fact, Detroit resembles a sort of modern Pompeii, except that here the lava wouldn't be molten rock, but rather the credit and debt that caused the urban exodus. This raises a question: Where did all the people go, all the people who left behind their dogs and brimming trashcans, the swings in their yards, which on a windy night will fool you into thinking that the kids have come back?

When spring comes to Detroit, what you can do is take a car ride past Eight Mile Road to the banks of Lake Saint Clair, or a stroll along the Wayne County Port Docks to watch the cargo ships returning up the big lakes under the Ambassador Bridge—long ships that will surely never see the ocean, but sometimes look as if that is where they are, because in the middle of Lake Erie or Lake Michigan, you'd think you were at sea, so much so that the gusts make the waves as choppy as in the Atlantic. The locks are what make the giant leaps between the lakes, and the channels are where the freighters languish, filled with wheat or coal. In Detroit, you'd sometimes think you were in a sea port, about to see a Nantucket whaling boat loom into view, because other than large oil tankers floating on the waves, you can see everything else on the big lakes: yachts, cargo ships, large sailboats, fishing boats, old sailing boats, motorboats.

It's against this backdrop that we meet Dwayne Koster for the first time, not actually on the shores of the big lakes, but in the suburbs of Detroit, at the steering wheel of an old 1969 Dodge Coronet, without us knowing right away why he's there, in his car, looking like a cop on patrol, cruising the streets, unsure what exactly he's looking for. That is until, rather quickly, we see him pull up on one of those long roads that extends from east to west for ten miles or so, where the city is already fading, giving way to large trees overhanging the houses. This is the first scene of my book: a guy parked in a white car with the engine off, in the wintry chill, with the attributes of his life slowly taking shape: a bottle of whiskey on the passenger seat, a mound of cigarette butts spilling from the ashtray, various magazines on the backseat (a fishing one, of course, a baseball one, of course), and a copy of *Walden* in the trunk, along with a hockey stick.

Sitting there, at the wheel of his old Dodge, he stares at the lit-up windows of a house, on whose mailbox we can read the name Fraser. Although we don't know it yet, Fraser is his ex-wife's last name, and therefore we don't know what it means to Dwayne Koster, parked there as evening falls, but there are sufficient clues and his agitation is such that what we do know is that he isn't there for no reason.

He could have spent hours on watch there in the snow that caked the wheels—I wrote—shielded from the dogs that came to cock their legs up against the door. He sat in such solitude that you would have said he was playing a role in some Finnish film, given the cold that chapped his lips, his parka, his gloves, which no longer sufficed (since there was no question of leaving the engine running for the heater), and, at this point in his life anyway—from what we also understand—given the fact that this is what he wanted, to be stung by the cold and snow and chilled to the bone.

When we met him at the beginning of the book, it must be said that Dwayne Koster had seemed removed from normal life, if a normal life is what he'd tried to construct over the last twenty years, and which now ran through his fingers like sand; if a normal life henceforth meant vanished images of his old home, his two kids, Tim and Dorothy, a happy life with Susan, and memories of a honeymoon at Niagara Falls (Room 207 of the Bristol Hotel, with the mist coming through the window).

But all of this—I wrote—all of these things that he now saw again, as if in a dream, through the windshield of his Dodge, were shut off, so to speak, in a distant place, an old life which lingered on his face only as irremovable mourning. There, lost in the Michigan night—I continued—the only thing that comforted Dwayne Koster was to put his favorite Jim Sullivan album on the car CD player and listen to songs like "Highways" or "UFO" on repeat, telling himself it was a shame that the entire world didn't listen to a singer like him, and that it was also a shame that Jim Sullivan himself had disappeared under such strange circumstances.

I don't know whether now is the time to bring this up, but the fact is that there are still a lot of mysterious things about Jim Sullivan's disappearance, which occurred about forty years ago in the New Mexican desert. They found his car at the edge of the desert, but they never found his body or any trace of a struggle, only his Coccinelle parked near Santa Rosa, its doors and windows closed, and without even the slightest damage or sign of forced entry. It's true that in America, especially when a singer is a bit mystical and his best-known song is called "UFO," this type of thing will lead certain fans to believe, without a doubt, that Jim Sullivan was abducted by aliens. Others allude to a settling of scores by the local mafia, still others to police error. Either way, it's true that the disappearance of Jim Sullivan remains a mystery, one that naturally fascinated Dwayne Koster. Otherwise, I wouldn't have titled my book *The Disappearance of Jim Sullivan*.

But Dwayne Koster had other things to think about besides Jim Sullivan when, behind the curtains of 224 Romeo Street, he saw the silhouette of Susan Fraser appear, the same silhouette which, for a long time, to Dwayne's regret, had borne the surname Koster, before she reverted to her maiden name. It was precisely this sort of thing that made him drink a little more. His eyes stung from the overpowering tobacco smoke inside the car, or possibly just from the excess of everything in his body, given that the bottle of whiskey sitting in the passenger seat hadn't been full for quite some time.

Seeing him there in the snow which melted before his eyes, it would have been difficult to believe that this was the same man who for twenty years had put on a well-pressed suit, a white shirt, and a rather colorful tie every morning before heading off to the University of Michigan. For, he was a professor at that university.

I also noticed that in American novels, one of the main characters was always a university professor, often at Yale or Princeton, but whatever the case, a college with a name revered throughout the world—although for my part, I spent a long time figuring out where Dwayne Koster would teach before realizing that he lived in Detroit, so it was logical that he'd have a job at the nearest university. Which, as I discovered, was in Ann Arbor, the name of a small town in the suburbs of Detroit, and also an excellent university, although not quite as prestigious as Berkeley or UCLA.

What I pictured right away in Ann Arbor was Dwayne Koster's big office, with books lining every wall, a view of the clipped campus lawn, and dozens of students who'd just sat down in a lecture hall dressed like Americans, with plaid shirts and Converse sneakers, and who at the end of class came to ask Dwayne questions about literature, because although I haven't yet mentioned it, Dwayne Koster taught literature. American literature, of course. He'd even written his PhD thesis on the influence of *Moby-Dick* on the contemporary novel—although I never overly dwelled on that for fear of becoming tedious. On the frosted glass pane of his office door, like the ones in police stations that you see in movies, was engraved his name: Dr. Dwayne Koster.

Chapter 3

Later, I tried to understand why I had named him Dwayne Koster, but I couldn't figure it out. I know only that one day in June, while looking at the map of the United States hanging on the wall of my office, this was the name that came to me. Dwayne Koster was the name that I attached to that silhouette on the streets of Detroit. And I told myself that that was it. With that name I could start putting something together, and along with it, everything else took shape at practically the same time: Jim Sullivan and his old Dodge, his ex-wife Susan, and Detroit, the same city where he was to become an average Joe, or rather a damned soul who'd personify all the city's tragedies and ruins. Dwayne, however, wasn't born in Detroit or any part of Michigan, but at the other end of the country, in Florida, near the swamps that border the Gulf of Mexico, after which his family moved to the Far North, or at least what he as a child perceived to be the Far North: the large, frozen lakes of Wisconsin, in contrast to the humid heat of Tallahassee.

Most of the time, it's the opposite that happens: people leave Michigan to go to Florida. They exchange the muddy snow of the North for the tropical sweetness of Daytona Beach, so much so that Florida has become the oldest state in the United States, which is to say, the average age is the highest there, given that in general, people retire to Florida when they're around sixty years old and die slowly after a final facelift at a luxury clinic. But the Kosters did the exact opposite, which was even more the opposite in 1962, when—according to what I read—people started to leave Detroit in earnest. At least the Whites fled the city and its instability in droves well before the riots of '67, which were later to wreak havoc on the city, well before the automobile factories tried to conceal the violence on the streets and the city's decline by manufacturing shinier and more muscular cars, such as the Dodge Coronet that Dwayne was to drive on Michigan's roads thirty years later.

So, Dwayne Koster crossed the United States from south to north one day in 1962. His father, Donald, was at the steering wheel of his large, yellow Buick Skylark; Moll, his wife, was at his side; and Dwayne was sitting in the back, watching the Florida heat fade into the distance, until they stopped for the night at a rather deserted motel in Georgia, where they ate very greasy French-fries and Moll felt the need to scour the shower cubicle before entering it—I dwell on certain details not because they're significant in themselves, but because I've noticed that you don't write an American novel without paying keen attention to detail; the grubbiness of the shower and the squeakiness of the light switch and the moonrays that fell on Dwayne's uneasy face had to be like arrows that I shot straight at the reader's heart.

In that room where he was unable to fall asleep—I wrote—the only thing that delighted Dwayne was that they were moving closer to Auntie Joyce, Moll's sister, who lived in Chicago, and that henceforth they wouldn't miss eating the Thanksgiving turkey together since, from Detroit to Chicago, if the traffic wasn't too bad, it took about five hours at most, almost shorter than going to Niagara Falls; obviously, Dwayne was familiar with the Falls only from the postcard pinned to the fridge with a magnet that the same Auntie Joyce had sent them three years earlier, on whose back was written something like this: "Lee and I send our love. The falls are magnificent, it's the only place in the world worthy of a honeymoon."

And this wasn't just a detail, since it is thanks to this postcard that we hear about Lee Matthews for the first time in my story. Well, Lee Matthews was an important character in my book, not only because it was thanks to him that Dwayne had met Susan, not only because Dwayne had owed him big time since that Saturday in March 1975, but because thanks to Lee, he'd ran into Susan for the first time in the bar of the Norton Shores Yacht Club, on the seashore—I mean to say, on the shore of Lake Michigan, but everyone there calls it the ocean. But this isn't the moment to talk about Lee Matthews, since he entered the story somewhat later in the plot. In this sort of book, certain characters are best left for later in the story. The only thing that mattered in the beginning was that it was Lee who actually introduced Dwayne to Susan, after which they saw each other quite frequently and started going for walks together, then fell in love, then got married, and all the other cascading things that you find in American novels.

And then getting divorced.

And then being on a stakeout a few hundred yards from her house, asking himself every night what he'd accomplished in his normal, American life. Nothing, nothing at all, he replied to himself, continuing to chew over his life beneath the acacias, which thawed gradually as the days passed, while Jim Sullivan belted out his ballads on the radio and children circled his old Dodge like flies.

Once in a while, sitting there on Romeo Street, he'd eject the Jim Sullivan CD and turn on the radio as if to help remind himself that there was a world that continued to turn. Especially since in that world, in the spring of 2003, whether in Michigan or the middle of New Hampshire, it was the beginning of the Iraq War—the type of event that can't be passed over in silence when you're American, which is to say, an American author. This type of event, which hovers over books, can involve the characters in the problems of their times. It's one of those things you come across in America, the presence of recent events that have actually taken place, like the destruction of the Twin Towers, or the financial crisis, or the invasion of Iraq. These are the things that have to hit the characters like a shockwave, so that even an American like Dwayne Koster, at one time or another, must have been preoccupied by the Iraq War—not directly, of course, but let's say indirectly. And that's what happened. Later in my book, that's what would happen.

Now the kids got out their bikes, asking each other who was the guy sitting over there on their street under the bare trees. Some of the more daring kids pressed their noses against the window and peered inside at Dwayne's face, which didn't look back at them. His eyes were fixed on the curtains of 224, because he'd noticed another silhouette behind the curtain—not just Susan's or the kids', but the silhouette of a man who seemed to be at home there, in Susan Fraser's kitchen—the same silhouette which, two hours earlier, holding a bouquet, had barely taken the time to wipe his feet on the WELCOME of the doormat.

If we were to judge by Dwayne's face and knowing his thoughts in that moment, it wasn't a good idea for the man in question to be in that place, or any place really, so Dwayne thought—as we soon discovered that Dwayne knew him, and we also discovered that he taught at the same university, at least he did when Dwayne taught there. If I may say so right now, when the story began, it had been a long time since he Dwayne had set foot on campus—for reasons that I'll take the opportunity to explain later—and, maybe due to which—I really mean maybe—the man in question wasn't a stranger.

But anyway, to return to the guy behind the window: Dwayne never really liked him. He was the kind of slightly arrogant colleague that you say hello to in the hallway, forcing a smile, the kind who you tell yourself must have been on the football team when he was a kid, and the kind who Dwayne secretly hoped would never obtain a tenured position at Ann Arbor, that he would soon go back to whence he came, which is to say his little university in Minnesota, with his little football team and those petite majorettes. But of course, that wasn't what would happen.

The fact is that even though Dwayne was no longer officially Susan's husband, even though a thousand things had happened since their separation, there was no way he would have been able to handle it if it were Alex Dennis—Alex Dennis, yes, that was his name, also engraved on the frosted pane of his office in the university's English Department—if it were Alex Dennis, as I was saying, who had just wiped his feet on Susan's doormat, holding a bouquet of flowers.

Chapter 4

In Detroit, Susan Fraser, too, was reflected 3,200 times in the windows of the city. Susan, too, lived in that disturbing city so full of promises, with her daughter Dorothy, whom she took to school in the morning in her 4x4 Toyota, after making toast for Tim. Essentially, all the things to do with everyday life in America. In that middleclass, even quite well-to-do, America, you had to settle into a routine and suppress all weariness; the weariness of an unfulfilled life that you could see clearly on the wrinkled bodies at the gym where Susan typically went twice a week, since she was always rather athletic and took care of herself at the gym and jogging park.

In the past she'd even played a lot of tennis, battling the strong gusts of wind from the wide plains of Michigan, collecting medals that were then tossed into a forgotten drawer, because it had been a long time since she gave it up. She would bat a ball around once in a while at the Sterling Heights Country Club before the move to Rochester Hills, which wasn't as nice as Sterling Heights, given that Sterling Heights was the nicest place in Detroit—based on what I've read, Sterling Heights is actually the sixth safest city in the United States.

I don't know how they calculate that kind of thing, but the fact is that Sterling Heights, with its 60,000 inhabitants, isn't seventh or fifth, but sixth, while Rochester Hills, as calm and enormous as any other suburb in North America, isn't even on the list. So, Susan had found a house in Rochester for a good price, somewhere in the neighborhood of $150,000, all the way at the end of Romeo Street. That made her smile: Romeo Street, with the court decision granting her divorce still echoing in her ears.

The point is that she could clean her 4x4 there, on the white paved stone driveway that led to the garage, she could give Tim and Dorothy each their own room, and she could greet the neighbors with a nod of the head until she got to know them better. In Sterling Heights during all those years with Dwayne, they'd had the time to get to know their dozen or so neighbors, with whom they'd held so many big barbecues, the Garrets and the Ambersons, during the countless hours she'd spend peeling vegetables and cutting them into strips for the hors-d'œuvres, and during the poker nights spent with George Radcliffe and, in particular,

Ralph Amberson, back when Dwayne hadn't been afraid of losing his fifty-dollar buy-in.

They obviously had thousands of memories of laughter during the endless summers and winters, of shoveling snow while talking about the kids, of Halloweens when, no matter what their disguise, she'd know which kid was asking her for which piece of candy, and of the notes about the flowers that they asked Ralph and Becky to water while they were away in Florida every year for Easter. But that was then. Now, the neighbors didn't know what flowers she grew in her garden, and—as I was increasingly led to believe—she had neither the time nor the desire to garden, or even to get to know her neighbors.

Susan and her ravaging smile. Susan and her five and a half feet. Susan and her dark eyes. Even if I'm not going over the top describing the characters' physical features, I can't help but mention Susan's dark eyes, as deep as a volcanic lake, and her curly hair, also dark, and long, rather like Sigourney Weaver's. She was the kind of girl that you could imagine in a Renaissance Center office, managing the sales department of an automobile firm, as easily as you could picture her at a punk concert at the Masonic Temple, especially a punk concert at the Masonic Temple.

I was born too late to be a part of the punk movement but one of the first things I thought to myself was that it would be good for a character to have been a punk while growing up in Detroit, maybe even to have fallen in love at an Iggy Pop concert. Then a little later, having matured over the years, the character would honeymoon at Niagara Falls. That's exactly what happened to Susan Fraser. The first time she kissed Dwayne Koster was the day of the legendary Iggy Pop concert at the Masonic Temple on March 23, 1977, without knowing that she was going to become his wife, let alone the mother of his children, or that they'd spend their honeymoon in the mist of the Falls, or that twenty years later she'd regret it. In any case, she didn't know that in time, things would fall apart—definitely not their love, or the feeling of love, which was surely anchored in a far-off time and place (in Iggy Pop's eyes somewhere at the Masonic Temple), but maybe the obviousness of being together or the possibility of being together would fall apart due to the cracks in their relationship, which grew too wide too quickly to be repaired.

It must be said that Dwayne had a flaw: he drank too much. To be fair to him, he had an excuse: he'd fought in Vietnam. Even though his worst memories were from a training camp in Ohio, even though he'd thanked Nixon a hundred times for having put an end to the madness just as he was boarding the plane, he remembered plenty of hours lying in the mud with a vicious corporal pressing his gun to the back of his neck saying: "Crawl, Koster, crawl," so that years later he continued to squander his nights with shots of Jack Daniels and in burning insomnia, which cracked the walls of the brain.

So, the cracks turned into holes that Susan no longer tried to fill, the same holes whose size Dwayne regretted in his car as he continued to surveil her comings and goings, with which he was all too familiar.

She knew that he was there, but she didn't say anything as long as he didn't cross the legal boundary that she had obtained before the judge, the two-hundred-yard exclusion zone that obliged him to use binoculars in order to observe them.

He saw everything as clearly as could be. He saw Alex Dennis's laugh, his broad gestures, and all of his other traits that he'd put up with dozens of times in the university hallways when he saw Alex marching around with a student, quoting Jack Kerouac or William Burroughs, as he was a specialist in the Beat Generation. Obviously, Dwayne thought, it was more glamorous than *Moby-Dick*.

As he thought back over this and that, the thousands of other things that had cast a shadow on his life, it all acted like a chemical reaction that crystallized as he sat in his old, white Dodge, which was slightly dirty from the winter. There in his head, expressions too lucid for the reader emerged—some of the most violent, the clearest expressions that the children could read from his lips through the car window, expressions like *fils de pute* or *trou de cul* in French, words that sound better in American English: "motherfucker," "asshole." They were the kinds of words that suggested unfinished business between people, and even suggested that this business, sooner or later, would have to be dealt with.

Except that we learned nothing more about it in the beginning. On the other hand, the problem remains, held in suspense at the end of a chapter, and we have to wait for the next part in order to understand how we arrived here.

Even though I don't really like flashbacks, I knew that it would come down to that. In regard to American novels, it's impossible to avoid flashbacks, including pointless ones—often there are whole pages about the protagonist's mother or father, who's been dead for a long time. So much so that you end up forgetting that you're in the past; so much so that when you return to the present, it seems to be the other way around, which is to say, it's the main character who no longer has a purpose. Personally, I tried to avoid drawing out the character's past for an eternity, but even so, there are things that must be told, things to do with Dwayne Koster, his origins, and, if I may say so, his cracks.

Part II

Chapter 1

WHEREAS THE MAYFLOWER had already crossed the Atlantic thirty years previously, a certain Johannes Hendrick Koster was to leave the Netherlands in 1652, on a merchant ship that would take him to the East Coast of the United States within the span of a few weeks—but only after weathering two storms, making a stopover in Newfoundland, and finally sending a small boat ashore, having anchored off what was then called New Amsterdam.

The sole heir of a rich family of Dutch drapers, the young, impulsive Johannes would have been ruined had he stayed in the other Amsterdam—the old one, that is—having invested his family fortune in the expanding horticultural market, and the tulip market in particular. The first bulbs had just arrived from Turkey and were all the rage; so much so that in 1637, within a few months the price of tulips took off in a completely irrational way and consequently provided a fashionable stock-market opportunity for adventurous investors—Johannes Koster leading the charge—who expected to reap one hundred times their investment. But Johannes Hendrick, like his friends, was about to fall a helpless victim to the first stock market crash in the history of the West. The same year, in 1637, after the tulip bulbs reached the exorbitant sum of 2,500 florins, the price suddenly collapsed. Over the following days, dozens of speculators disappeared or drowned themselves in the North Sea, more out of shame than because they were ruined. The whole episode affected all of Europe and made more than one person smile.

Having fallen into a state of deep neurasthenia, Johannes could sometimes be found treading the cobblestones of Amsterdam's port, a prophetic ghost warning young pilgrims against their delusions of the New World. But one day, said Dwayne's grandmother, when he was still only forty, he made eye contact with the beautiful Bethsabee on the docks. Legend has it that he regained his will to live and his sense of adventure and took her to the West Indies. They came ashore on the coast of New Holland a few weeks later and started a family, from which they, the Kosters of America, were all directly descended.

You, too, Dwayne, his grandmother stressed, you're an American Koster, too. Your life, too, will fluctuate from high to low and low to high. She'd thank heaven that she was American and always said mystical things about their country.

She, Abigail was her name, was from a small town in Alabama. She always said that the only major thing ever to have happened there was when The Wild West Show passed through in 1901, at which she saw Sitting Bull and Buffalo Bill in the flesh, with her own eyes. But she said that what stuck with her the most was the Annie Oakley act—the fastest gun the West, who shot the ashes off her husband's cigarette from eighty feet away, on her first bullet. Abigail Koster had managed to retrieve the seven of clubs playing card that Annie Oakley had shot in two from a distance of more than a hundred feet.

I didn't write about any of this in my book. I simply drew portraits of my characters the better to understand them, including the most secondary of characters. I kept records. That's how I knew all those things about Johannes Koster. That's how I knew all those things about Abigail. That's how I knew, for example, that Dwayne's father was a Democrat. That's how I knew, to take another example, that Moll Koster, Dwayne's mother, had had a lover—however, I did mention that in my book, given that it concerned Dwayne, since he had surprised the lover in question in his mother's bed when he was barely ten years old. And it wasn't just any day, but a day that we find cited in every pre-September 11, 2001 American novel. By which I mean November 22, 1963.

Dwayne—if I may share this here—was watching TV when his favorite show was interrupted to inform America that President Kennedy had died in Dallas that noon, from a bullet to the head that had killed him instantly. So, obviously, upon hearing this news, Dwayne leapt from the sofa and rushed upstairs, quickly enough for his steps to resound, thereby warning the lovers. But their passion, their furtiveness, or all the things that biblically joined them right then meant that they didn't hear the child's heavy footfalls; so, without any warning, Dwayne opened the door, entered the room, and stood right in front of the bed where, despite their adultery, they didn't hide themselves under the sheets. They were therefore butt naked and, in a manner of speaking, indulging one another. They were there, frozen and winded in almost complete darkness while the child stood in the doorway saying nothing, not even that John Fitzgerald Kennedy was no longer alive.

Then, it was as if the man's silhouette moved in the dark and Dwayne found himself in the violent shadow of a man that he didn't know. Suddenly dominating him and standing up, he screamed: "You punk. Get out of here you moron or I'll kill you!" And, from that voice like a gaping tunnel, Dwayne backed away, out onto the landing, and ran just as quickly back down the stairs.

Later, he remembered that that day he'd run through the countryside with the voice seemingly chasing him through the forest, beneath the scratching branches, until he collapsed out of breath on a riverbank and fell asleep on the wet grass. He remembered that his mother bent over him a few hours later and told him that he'd been dreaming, that he'd apparently had a nightmare. He believed her for a little while. If President Kennedy hadn't actually been dead, he probably would have believed her still.

Chapter 2

It's true that there were more students who regularly took seminars with Alex Dennis than with Dwayne Koster. And it's true that it made Dwayne's hair stand on end when Alex took it upon himself to tell him that he should be spending more time on research, and other such harsh remarks as you find in campus novels—not that I thought for a second about writing a campus novel; but because certain characters were part of the university, there were obviously remarks like that, remarks that could be made next to the coffee machine in the staff room, where Alex always arrived before Dwayne, smiling at him with his big pearly whites and seven extra inches of height.

All of this would have been far in the past had Alex Dennis gone back to Minnesota like he was supposed to and had he not gotten a job at Ann Arbor. It would have been even farther away if, the same year when Alex Dennis was looking for a house in the Detroit suburbs, an American magazine hadn't published a list of the safest cities in the United States, ranking Sterling Heights sixth.

Dwayne saw the trailer parked there on Beaver Street, the black GMC in front of it, and the tall blonde girl in high heels who got out of it, who seemed to be warning her husband that she wouldn't be lifting a single box the entire day—she was how old? twenty-nine or thirty, you might have said a bit older because of her makeup, or maybe even because of her being upset about leaving Minnesota that day. As if you could be upset about leaving Minnesota, Dwayne had thought: Louisiana I'd understand, Massachusetts, sure, but not Minnesota.

But against all odds, Dwayne would soon have the chance to tell Kimberly this himself, in his own garden, since, out of politeness or masochism—in either case, under the pretext of their being colleagues and neighbors—Susan thought that was the done thing. Yes, you invite them over for dinner, that's what you do. Susan insisted and consequently convinced Dwayne that one Saturday or another, he'd have to put up with Alex Dennis over dinner at their table in their home.

To be honest, I thought for a long time that my book would start here—at that big dinner that would put all of the characters in one place and provide a real idea of America—thanks to the countless novels I'd read that commence like that: in the middle of a big scene in which nothing happens, but which allows everyone to be introduced.

For a long time, I reflected on what an American author would have done with that dinner in Michigan's white America, with Dwayne, who'd grill two kilos of beef on the back porch, with the smell of the pines and conversations about baseball, with Ralph and Becky joining them so that Dwayne wouldn't feel so lonely. For a long time, I thought about the kinds of pages an American author would have written, just following Susan from four in the afternoon as she peeled carrots, scooped guacamole into small bowls, and checked on the eggplants, while Dwayne, wearing Bermuda shorts, out in the garden, got ready to light the barbecue. I ended up—given that sooner or later, yes, of course, I would be obliged to be like an American novelist—actually describing the cocktails in their glasses and every object in the kitchen, from the KichenAid that Susan was given at Christmas to the garden nook that Dwayne had built with his own hands. Yes, his own hands, Susan repeated as she gave Kimberly a tour of the house, the way you do in the United States, more often than you do in France, where women give tours of their house while the men sit in their deckchairs and try to find something in common.

But even so, Dwayne said, it's crazy that despite

the incredible 1984 season, Lance Parrish still hasn't made the Hall of Fame. His time will come, Ralph replied as he dropped an ice cube in his glass and regretted the Tiger's career, which, for the past twenty years, had been going relentlessly downhill.

It must be said that of all the years in which my story unfolded, of all the years in which Dwayne Koster could have shared with Ralph Amberson the memory of seeing the Tigers' batter knock a ball to the bleachers, of all the years in which he could have hit a homerun as legendary as the one in the New York Polo Grounds in 1951, the Tigers had now hit a rough patch, without the smallest trophy and without the least legendary match. So, for Dwayne, Ralph, and all Tigers fans, all that was left was to remember better days, when they'd even won the World Series four times: in 1935, 1945, 1968, and 1984. Especially in 1984, Dwayne recalled, when they'd beaten the San Diego Padres, with talented players like Lance Parrish and Kirk Gibson, who to this day, from what I've read, hit the most beautiful homerun of the season—the same homerun that Dwayne—I wrote—had seen over and over again in his dreams, its marvelous arcs akin to the ball-like comets of the Milky Way.

If the batter—I wrote—hits the ball out of the park, if no player on the other team can catch it, and if said batter can then run the three bases of the diamond (that's what the part of the field in question is called) before returning to the home plate (that's what the starting position of the batter is called), while every other baseman moves along in the same direction—if all of that happens, then yes—it's a home run.

But it must be said that the phenomenon had been rare since 1984. Since then, Dwayne, like Ralph, had had time to thank heaven that he lived in Detroit, which is to say, the city where the emblematic sport, the real glue between people, isn't baseball but ice hockey.

Of course, for us in France, it's a bit odd for us to put an ice hockey team in a book because we then think about Chambery or Annecy, and we don't really often think about telling stories that take place in those cities; what I mean is cities where it would be plausible for there to be a hockey team—although I did discover that there's even a hockey team in Brest. That's something I never would have guessed, because it's still a violent sport, an extremely savage sport, which fits well with a specific image of America, and, in my opinion, less so with a specific image of Bretagne. It's a sport that fits well with guys like Dwayne Koster, if, like Americans, you think that demons are exorcized through sports, even more so if you think that Dwayne Koster is a more complex and darker character than he seems and that like many other Americans, there are volcanoes dormant in his head—the types of volcanoes that can erupt at any moment.

But on the evening of the barbecue, they didn't erupt. On the contrary, everything was mellowed by alcohol, and Susan silently thanked Ralph for constantly negotiating the distance that separated Dwayne and Alex Dennis.

I often thought that things like this are what the American novelist would have written. I mean, not only the smell of the pine trees in the clear night, not only the rustling of the maples in the evening breeze, but what was decipherable in the furrows on everyone's brows, in the anxiety on their lips, and what was going on in their minds: the passing thoughts and forbidden desires, there, in the Koster's garden. The way Becky bent over when she helped Susan set the table—you would have said that she calculated precisely from which poorly fastened button you would be able to glimpse the inner curve of her breasts. The way Alex smiled at Becky Amberson with a hint of awkwardness. The way Susan looked at her bending over so that you could read on her, Susan's, face—in the blink of an eye that brought her to Alex's elusive gaze—so that you could read not who Becky was, not who Alex was, but maybe who Susan was. And all the other things that require pages and pages so that we'll be able to understand what is going to happen, or so that we'll think we know what is going to happen, since certain things won't occur, but others will.

Chapter 3

STILL, FOR SOME time, in Dwayne's head, under the illuminated leaves of the maple trees, Alex Dennis remained like a jigsaw piece that would finally insert itself in its proper place all on its own. At which point, at the end of the get-together, it wasn't Ralph but Dwayne himself who proposed the next get-together to Alex. They could play poker, next week for example, said Dwayne, deeming it a good idea to have a fresh partner, a guy who'd told them he didn't play often, in which case they would be glad to show him the ropes. The next day, when Ralph and Dwayne were together, they said to each other that once you got past appearances, the guy was actually nice.

And then the following week, all four of them met in Dwayne's basement, converted for poker games, with its felt-covered table, four glasses already filled, and, above all else, permission to smoke inside, which Susan granted her husband once a month on the condition that he didn't lose more than fifty dollars during the game.

So, as usual, they played Texas Hold'em: two cards face up on the table, you buy the other three by doubling the stake, and if someone raises and you agree, everyone else must see the bet before going back around. Next, it's like normal: you pay to see, you raise, or you fold when you want. Good, they fully agreed, they played the same game, they subscribed to the same magazine, and they watched the same championship on TV.

So, maybe as simply as that, they shouldn't have opened the second bottle of brandy. Maybe they should have known that by breaking one rule, they'd break them all. Till one in the morning. Fifty dollars max. Half a pack of cigarettes. Only one bottle. It was all smashed to pieces when Alex won and Dwayne refused to relinquish the fifty dollars that belonged to him.

But the problem with poker is that to win back fifty dollars, the first thing you have to do is put fifty dollars back in the game, so that very quickly in the center of the table under the strong light that illuminated the felt tabletop, written on a piece of paper, there already lay three hundred dollars. Dwayne had placed the bet hoping that Alex would fold, that he would prefer to lose the one hundred dollars he'd already invested rather than another two hundred.

What really matters, Dwayne thought, is that he won't leave with my fifty dollars.

Except that he said all of this to himself while running his middle finger over his lips. Without him knowing that during the previous hands it had been odd, Alex told himself, he hadn't done it before—as he would explain to Dwayne later—you see, I saw right away, Alex told Dwayne, that you didn't have a play, I saw it right away because if you had really had a play, you would have touched your wedding ring, meaning that you would have done it, he continued to explain, in order to prevent us from thinking you had a play, and, significantly, to avoid scratching your arm, since you tried to make me believe the whole evening that your tell was to scratch your arm; so, you knew very well that by doing that, I'd think you had a play, I mean, if you thought you were doing the opposite of what you'd normally do, and as for me, I know that you will do the opposite one way or another, so I knew what you were doing. And he'd jumbled it all up like that, the way only he knew how and, as Dwayne was to learn, the way he knew how all too well.

But at that moment, no. At that moment, Dwayne knew nothing except that he'd made a new friend and that after all, it's not every day in the complicated life of a man in your forties that you make new friends.

Anyway, at one point in the evening, Dwayne

still got up, threw his cards on the table, in debt to the tune of more than four hundred dollars, and said: I give up. Four hundred dollars, Dwayne thought later, that's an expensive new friend.

But worse still was that Susan found out about it. Four hundred dollars. She was more upset than her husband and thought that the whole neighborhood already knew about it, so she avoided Beaver Street. She even avoided her usual supermarket lest she run into Kim and have to put on a face, something to hide the shame or pride that she feared that could be read in her looks. So, over nervous evenings and tense conversations in the bosom of his home, Dwayne opened up to Ralph, who himself had spoken about it to Alex; and that was too stupid, since the whole business about four hundred dollars spoiled the whole neighborhood. So, one afternoon, when Dwayne wasn't home, Alex went to ring Susan's doorbell and sort it all out.

No one will ever know what his intentions were deep down inside that day, but the official reason was that he had come to return the four hundred dollars and apologize to a wife for having cleaned out her husband at poker.

For Susan, the two options that she thought she had were either to slam the door in his face, or ask him inside, taking his hands in her own and dragging him to the couch—deep down she didn't really hesitate.

In the end, that's possibly why I came, he told her an hour later, naked in her marital bed, reconstructing the events that had led them there, thinking about Becky's shirt on the evening they first met, and everything that those two already knew when late in the evening they'd taken their tour of the garden, behind the shrubs and the rhododendrons—all things I'd described in detail during the barbecue scene, so that that we already knew what was going to happen; even if we still didn't know which of the two, Becky Amberson or Susan Koster, was going to fall into Alex's arms, but every word already exchanged between the two, Alex and Susan, had made manifest the signs of desire.

But in the end, nothing had happened that evening. In front of the red-hot coals of the barbecue, nothing had happened; or rather nothing except the growing feeling of knowing that it was going to happen, given that people who meet and tacitly become attracted to each other—like Alex and Susan—know from the start how it'll end, and they know how they'll end up changing the story about how they met while gazing into each other's eyes as their heads rest on a pillow.

What no two lovers ever bring up on any pillow, and the subject that lingers in every adulterous bedroom, however, is what that does to each of their heads after the love and the illicitness, after the bed has been made and the door closed once more, so that each of them can go back to their own lives. For example, what it did to Susan, who just put the four hundred dollars on the table by the entrance, waiting for Dwayne's return, who busied herself in the kitchen, waiting to make eye contact as he took off his coat in the hallway, who smoothed her skirt with her hand one hundred times to erase every last trace of her infidelity, with the so new and painful feeling of having planted a bomb under her life—a bomb that she took with her to every room of the house, wondering that evening, as she mentioned to Dwayne that Alex had brought the four hundred dollars, when it would explode.

So, the next day when Alex rang the doorbell again—already committing the craziness of holding a bouquet of flowers—the next day, she would open the door a little less than the day before and, gazing at him with her big, dark eyes, she would say, "No," she would say, "I'm sorry, no, I can't," and the many other similar things that one calls virtue or simply fragility.

And as she drew the bolt on her door, she was so relieved to have defused her bomb that she was a million miles from thinking that Dwayne had one in his life as well, a bomb primed to explode—a bomb named Milly Hartway.

Chapter 4

I WAS OFTEN unsure as to the order in which I should tell the whole story, given the different characters therein and thus the different narrative lines that would more or less end up intersecting each other but which would really require patience on the part of the reader. But I never doubted that this was how you wrote an American novel; especially if I wanted it to be like a saga, as it so often says on the back cover; "a true saga that winds through history" and the sort of utterly enticing sentence that explains the international appeal of a book.

Anyway, this was the moment that I chose, after Alex and Susan had, so to speak, begun and ended their relationship, for us to discover the other side of Dwayne's life, a side named Milly Hartway—Milly, yes, that's what was written on the nametag she had pinned to her white button-up shirt every evening, which she took off around midnight, and which she put on the shelf when leaving the Warren diner where she worked. I don't know why I always thought that all American waitresses were named Milly, that they wore a black skirt and a white button-up, and that they always had a bit of a stormy love life with the out-of-work guys that you find on the other side of the counter—the type of guy who promises for the umpteenth time that he'll never drink again and that this time it'll work out between them; the type that Dwayne was to end up resembling after a while, waiting there so that they could leave together in the night and share a motel, which happened from time to time.

I wrote entire pages about Dwayne and Milly, about their love as it blossomed in parking lots and during long walks under the pines. Over the weeks, they'd learned to sneak around, as you learn to do during the hidden hours far from the highways and service stations, until their first night in a Grand Rapids motel, far from civilization, where they could be certain that no one would recognize them. But it was better that no one recognize them, all the more so given that she was not only his waitress, not only the girl that placed his mug of coffee or a beer in front of him in the diner in Warren, but first and foremost, his student.

Yes, his student. She only worked in the Warren diner to make ends meet; it was a place where he'd never have set foot if thousands of signs hadn't already existed between them on the Ann Arbor campus, signs that brought them together. In his large office, she often came to sit in front of him without even hiding the gum she was chewing, smiling, showing the tattoo she had on her shoulder, all the while worrying about the grade she was going to get in her next exam.

So after a few months, by means of the silent looks and lingering smiles that crossed the lecture hall between them, they finally reduced the gap that separated the two sides of the stage until one evening—I wrote—she entered his office without knocking on the door and asked him, just like that, asked him if he could drive her to work because she was going to be late—no, not just like that; she didn't ask him just like that: first, she asked him to talk about literature (questions about the narrator of *Moby-Dick*), and then as time went on, because they left the building together speaking about the book, after a few minutes they tacitly approached his car in the campus parking lot (at the time it wasn't a Dodge, but a metallic Chrysler, better for a family, less literary as well). At which point she looked at her watch pretending to be shocked. She placed her hand over her mouth saying, "I'm late" and then she asked if he'd mind taking her to Warren. She was like that, Milly Hartway.

He said yes. And so, they rode the four-lane highway that took them to Warren. And they pulled up in the diner parking lot; except that when it was time to get out of the car, instead of opening her door and thanking him for the ride, there you have it, she put her hand on his thigh.

She was very pretty, Milly Hartway, and she was one of the only girls registered for his seminar. So, thought Dwayne, even that was a sign from heaven. And then he put his arm around her.

In Dwayne's mind, due to the almost thirty years between them, due to the mascara that made her eyelashes longer, Milly Hartway was like a lead wrecking ball that bowled over his brain—she was daring enough to wear a bellybutton piercing, cultured enough to read sophisticated books by Thomas Pynchon and Don DeLillo. And while smoking in the nude, as they did on motel beds, during the hours they were able to live that way, they talked about sex and literature, entwining like the two lovers they had now become, before putting everything in their lives back in place and each going back to their own things. Dwayne started to love Milly. And Milly started to love Dwayne. And their story resembled something from a book.

It's true, said Dwayne, that our story resembles something from a book. I'd say one by Jim Harrison, don't you think? And she answered no, that it was a story by a woman, a story by Laura Kasischke or Joyce Carol Oates. Or even one by Richard Ford, he thought, watching a moth get annoyed at the ceiling light. Maybe Alice Munro, she thought. No, I know, he continued, it's one by Philip Roth. He said this because of the stormy noises his head was making—on the one hand he was a man of reason, who taught at a university, but on the other he was like a wild, lustful beast, who had discovered sexuality too late—yes, it's by Philip Roth, said Dwayne. But since she didn't really like Philip Roth and absolutely wanted to have the last word, she said the only name that was off limits, the only name that would definitely render him quiet and pensive, she said William Faulkner.

And as he watched her, still naked, redoing her hair in the mirror, or as they both looked at the white Dodge for sale in the parking garage, every minute, he preferred not to think about the disaster that it would produce if one unlucky day their relationship leaked out—which is to say, if the bomb that he hung as a target over his body decided to explode.

Chapter 5

Obviously, it was going to happen. Obviously, of the two bombs that Susan and Dwayne were each separately holding, it was Dwayne's that was going to explode. It was his—I wrote—that an outsider would prime and then count down from ten to see the desired effect.

It was on her phone, Susan Fraser's (ten), as she drove along the four-lane highway that overlooked Downtown (nine). It probably surprised her to hear Becky's voice (eight), which seemed merely to be asking her how she was doing and purposefully avoiding a certain subject (seven) because she needed to say something (six). She quickly understood that she was putting off saying something serious or infuriating (five). And Susan, in the middle of the highway, phone pressed to her ear, tried to slow down (four), explaining that she couldn't talk long because she was driving (three). Of course,

Becky said, but even so, I need to tell you something . . . about Dwayne (two). And then she said it (one). She said: Milly Hartway.

And Susan silently pulled over onto the shoulder. She calmly put the phone on her knees, Becky's voice on the other end repeated her name, evaporating into thin air on the passenger's side. The gusts of air from the tractor trailers rushing past shook the car, while she instinctively activated the windshield washer, spreading a smell of alcohol indifferent to the first daffodils that invaded the nearby gardens.

Susan didn't say anything. She didn't ask if she was certain about what she said or how she had found out—I don't know, for example that a certain Alex Dennis had come across them by chance in an Ann Arbor parking garage, or that the same Alex Dennis had spent time with Becky Amberson, no, none of that, she, Susan, wasn't thinking anything about it.

She sat there, at the side of the highway, for maybe an hour; then she went home. That evening, she didn't say anything. The next day she said nothing, or even the day after that. There was maybe a bit of a silence over breakfast. She listened maybe a little less to the news on the radio. But she didn't say anything. Maybe it could last forever. Maybe every evening, she would flip a coin to see whether she'd tell him or not. And then one day, just like that, she told him. She feared doing it again and again, and then one day she did it. And it was all very simple.

She said: I don't want to see you any more. She said: get out, take your stuff, and leave. And perhaps the most curious thing is that Dwayne said nothing. He continued to stir his spoon in his mug without really even raising his head, like someone ready for it, like someone who could get up peacefully one morning, calmly leave the bedroom and go downstairs to the garage and, I don't know, sit in the driver's seat of his car and turn on the engine until the oxygen ran out. But that's not what he did.

No, that's not what he did, nor did he have any suicidal urge deep inside; unless we can also call what he did do a suicidal urge, namely filling two suitcases and driving into the morning sun, telling himself that he no longer lived there, that despite the so green grass or the so white house front, it was as if his house had now been invaded by termites, which he didn't know how to get rid of, and that it was necessary for him to go far away, to the other side of America, to Oregon maybe or North Dakota—and while he wasn't the type to go into exile, if going into exile meant piecing back together every element of his life one by one, with the whole series of decisions that that would entail; no, that was never Dwayne Koster. And even though I always made sure that Dwayne could evolve, even though I always held back from giving Dwayne Koster a chance, for the time being he'd have enough to do just to repair the fractures that currently prevented him from catching any glimpse of a stable and smiling future on the other side of the country; particularly at the age of forty-seven, in the United States circa 2000—even assuming that you run away to Mississippi or Alaska, even assuming that you're able to rewrite your past—you're not guaranteed to find a new job or even a new place to settle down.

You'd never really know why he did that in my novel, why he didn't lie or leave Milly straight away, why he got in his car with his suitcases filled with the few objects which, not for anything in the world, would he leave behind for Susan or anybody else: his copy of *Walden*, his The Stooges CDs, his hockey stick—yes, his hockey stick, because I told myself that it might come in handy; what I mean is, knowing that a rather hot-tempered guy like Dwayne goes around with a hockey stick in the trunk of his car, without knowing that it'd necessarily come in handy or how, but just that it was a possibility. A lot of things were like that in Dwayne's head: a possibility.

And as the sun rose, I wrote, Dwayne set out to drive around, drive around until a sea, a lake, or an empty tank decided for him where he should stop. He'd often done it before, he'd take his car to the first gas station, fill it up to the top, so that even his hands smelled of gas when he got back behind the steering wheel, and then decide to drive, to drive due west or south, following the green signs that already indicated the big cities like Denver or Chicago. The only thing that stopped him was an empty tank, like an old contract with himself, or even the only limitation that his brain was capable of finding; as if suddenly, when the engine began sputtering on Interstate 80, at the Iowa state line, his brain emerged from hypnosis, having just spent five or six hours on the smooth, bedspread roads, devoid of all countryside—nothing more in his memory than an abstract, pictorial representation of an America of skies and plains, if only America were something other than skies and plains, and the routes that cross them.

But this time, I continued, in the night that gathered up his soul, there was a sort of luminous point that shone on the horizon. This time, the day the road opened up to him, Dwayne Koster pointed himself due west, telling himself that maybe he'd find refuge there, exactly two hundred miles from Detroit, on the banks of Lake Michigan, with a certain Lee Matthews.

Chapter 6

I ALSO HAD a file on Lee Matthews. Middle class. East coast. Son of a Republican congressman. Grew up in Rhode Island. Lived in Chicago. Married to Moll Koster's sister, therefore Dwayne's uncle by marriage. Studied history at the University of Pennsylvania. In his youth, took part in archeological digs in the Middle East before sauntering into the world of antique dealing. Antique store in Chicago. Big network. Owns a villa in Norton Shores. Even a member of the area's yacht club. Without a doubt had a fling with Dwayne's mother. Maybe he was the one Dwayne surprised in his mom's bed on the day of Kennedy's assassination—although I didn't develop that in the end. It remains a possibility, of course, but I never developed it; even if Dwayne's dad was still suspicious of him, of Lee Matthews, and didn't really like him.

No, I don't really like the guy: that was exactly

what Donald Koster said. Maybe out of suspicion. Maybe because he was a Republican, whereas the last Republican president that the Kosters had supported was in all likelihood Abe Lincoln, and even if Lee was smart enough to avoid the subject when serving the brandy on Thanksgiving evenings, everyone knew it. Everyone knew that Lee Matthews was the son of a former Republican congressman and that he'd never denied his, as it were, Texan origins—I say Texan not because that was where he was really from, from Texas, but because I find that this is the best way of representing a family of Republicans; in any case, that's how I picture him: in his own kingdom, or ranch, near an oil well, under a quite harsh sun, which makes it necessary to keep your Stetson on your head, and speaking with a heavy accent. But Lee Matthews wasn't Texan at all, rather he was descended from the distinguished East Coast middle-class and spent his vacations in Connecticut before returning to New York in September. And maybe it was this East Coast side of him, sophisticated and charming, cultivated and elegant, that had led Dwayne to oppose his dad, so that henceforth the only person who was like a refuge was his Uncle Lee.

And Dwayne was pretty sure he'd find him, his Uncle Lee, at Norton Shores, the most distinguished yacht club in the Midwest—the type of place where you'd definitely run into the gentry of Illinois and

Michigan all in one place, if the whole gentry numbered about one hundred or one hundred fifty people, so tightly interwoven that no newcomer could feel welcome; in any case, no newcomer would dare to try and enter the club's hallowed grounds. And even less so would he dare to sit in the club chairs in front of the bay window that dominates the lakefront, where sixty-year-olds find it becoming to wear their faux skipper's hats while drinking brandy, discussing business despite it apparently being a weekend, their eternal navy-blue sweaters decorated with endless white anchors, their classic deck shoes barely faded by the sun—in any event, not weathered by the brine or sea air, unless it be the air they breathed there on the teak decks of the club.

And indeed, Lee Matthews was there, cultivating the personal and business networks he had been tightly weaving for the last forty years or so, ever since he set sail into the world of antiques, which is to say, ever since he opened a store in Chicago in the early sixties, ever since he started travelling the length and breadth of America to buy and sell everything he could get his hands on, since Lee Matthews's network stretched far beyond the Norton Shores yacht club.

No, it didn't end there, and it's of no small significance to the development of this story that in his shop on Clark Street, Chicago, among all the pieces that passed through there, some of them had made a lot longer trip than from the attics of Maine or South Carolina; for example, in the last few years, from Kabul and Baghdad had come antique vases and statues that had long resided peacefully in local museums and by geopolitical magic had travelled far enough to end up in the glass display cases of Lee Matthews's shop—I developed many such things at length in my book and at one point it would be good to touch on them again, because Dwayne Koster was to become rather attached to Lee Matthews's stories; precisely because he went seeking refuge in the arms of that somewhat shady yet at the same time welcoming uncle, as I wrote several times.

Overall very welcoming, as Dwayne felt the evening he entered the yacht club bar and discreetly seated himself on a stool as he waited for Lee to see him and come over. And Lee came over to him.

Over the whiskey Lee had ordered for him, Dwayne told him his story—perhaps even a bit more than his story, perhaps the feelings of bitterness and betrayal that went with it—about how he had left everything, about how he was now penniless, with nothing but a car and an attentive uncle, who had already ordered him a second whiskey and was telling him that he could count on him, that of course he could stay there, in his Norton Shores villa. But the best thing for Dwayne would be the small cabin he owned up north, near Lake Huron.

I don't know if it's geographically clear that they

were on the banks of Lake Michigan, two hundred miles west of Detroit, whereas the cabin was situated forty miles from Detroit, but farther north because Lake Huron is north of Lake Michigan. Generally speaking, I must say, it's always a problem to explain distances in a novel. If it were up to me, I'd publish a map of the region in my book, charting the characters' movements, just to make sure that everything is clear.

But to return to Dwayne: if he wanted, Lee Matthews would give him the keys and Dwayne could settle in there, in that place he never visited—the type of cabin you find very close to lakes, with the bare necessities inside, even a woodstove for the winter and professional fishing tackle, the type of place where even rich people go from time to time in order to commune with nature. And Dwayne accepted.

Next, they spoke about other things: about Susan of course, about Milly of course, a little about sex, and then, after three whiskeys, he couldn't stop himself, he had to speak of angry things; he had to talk about Alex Dennis because, to him it was certain, it was that son-of-a-bitch Dennis who had seen them together, him and Milly, that son-of-a-bitch Dennis who had told everyone what he saw. And if one day I see him again, said Dwayne, if one day I see him again.

But if there's a problem you can't fix, Lee

Matthews stressed, you can count on me. Even, I mean, if one day you have a problem with a person, I can take care of it, Lee emphasized, meaning I won't take care of it directly, but rather I'll do it in such a way that the problem will disappear, you understand, so that the pressure will be taken off your life. I can do that for you, Dwayne. And taking him by the shoulder, he insisted on it: that if he wanted to see the problem go away, all he had to do was call. He shouldn't hesitate; he knew some good people, some good contacts, Lee said, resting his hand on Dwayne's shoulder. Perhaps Dwayne didn't totally understand where he was going or what he was talking about, but he thanked him warmly for giving him a place to stay, even a small fishing cabin, even in the middle of nowhere.

Chapter 7

AND THEN SUDDENLY, everything calms down. We turn the page and, just like that, everything is quiet, like a placid sea that seems hesitant to set in motion again, while the warm sun spreads its particles of light everywhere, over the trees and flowers, over the water that flows past the round rocks, the pine needles that carpet the ground, and the larch forests that darken the day. Here are hours consecrated to nature, to the unending mountains and deserted plateaus, to the dense forests, to the treetops that sift the light, the oak branches roamed by squirrels, the prairie dogs weaving in and out of the clearings, the tree trunks gnawed by thousands of beavers busy reinforcing their dam; even the life of the insects seems to overflow, providing the foundation for everything else.

By the river—the water that flows there carves the bed of a sylvan, sometimes savage, sometimes sluggish river—a man sprawls on the bank, at the spot where there is a waterfall lit by the misty rays of the sun. His eyes are half closed and he seems to be asleep. He hears the steady rumble of the cascade flowing behind him, which almost chills the air and showers the flora. In that instant, he could see a deer standing over him, which had come to drink from the spring. He could admire his reflection in the clear water and meditate on that rare or mythical sight; yes, mythical is the word that best describes the American wilderness.

Dwayne knew it well, the wilderness of northern Michigan: the trout that leap from the rivers and the autumn colors that are borne away on the fresh water. He and Ralph had thousands of weekend memories with cases of beer in the Mercury station wagon and hours of meditating as they cast their lines in Saginaw Bay. Sometimes they even went to Canada to find fishing holes, given there were more fish in Canadian waters, as Ralph remarked, and so many species, such as black sturgeon, yellow perch, smallmouth bass, and sunfish; so many faceless names that issued from Ralph's mouth by the nighttime campfire, giving them the impression that they were one with nature, as if Native American spirits had begun to float on the air, yes, they said to each other, trembling, it was something wild and almost inhuman, when each sentence seemed to take the shape of a shamanic thought, as they talked about what it was like to piss from on top of a rock, and all the things that Dwayne had read a thousand times in a thousand novels, which had grown a little stale for him, he said, the campfires and the bears that rummage through the trashcans, in the novels, yes, it had grown a little stale for him. But in real life, it was what he needed, a little clear water and no one in sight. And then, of course, Milly Hartway. Of course, Milly Hartway.

As long as he put a little gas in the Dodge again, as long as he drove the forty miles that separated Port Huron from Warren, he still came to take his seat there, on the high stools of the diner where Milly still worked, around the countertop whose red dominated the whole space. Milly hadn't let him go, not yet. There, leaning his elbows on the counter, he waited for the noise of the vacuum, the buckets of water that around midnight she emptied beneath the slightly dimmed wall lights, he waited for her to finish making those noises or that gesture, so he could leave the diner and take her with him to the coolness of the cabin, where they slept in each other's arms on the damp mattress.

Milly, I wrote, swept the dead leaves a hundred times over the threshold of the door. Dwayne saw her bathe hundreds of times, fleeing the trees' shadows to hang her towel in the June sun, the sound of her bare feet on the floor boards, the contours of her body, which Dwayne watched through the grubby windowpanes, rather conscious of the fact that some day or other, she'd draw another line across her life, rather conscious of the fact that they wouldn't be able to fall together forever, that for her, life, literature, everything, would coalesce into one solid point from which he'd be excluded.

But not right away. Not at this point in the story. At this point in the story, no, she hadn't let him go, or even thought about it for a second. She was even thinking about finding him a job, no matter what, she said, but you're not going to teach at the university any more, you need to find something else. So, every day, between two coffees, she replied to job ads; every day she talked about Dwayne to customers at the diner: even the night watchman and a cashier in a parking garage. He was willing to do anything, Milly said.

It was rather intelligent of her not to repeat the violent things that Dwayne ruminated on all by himself, the dark phrases that skipped over the lake like flat pebbles, such as: "No one would want an old, alcoholic professor" and "real life is long gone"; she wanted to believe that in sayings like that, brazen and bottled up inside, there was the no-going-back portrait of the man that he'd become—the kind of man who may once have been either a university professor or a senator but finds himself there, in the trough of the wave, dreaming of one thing: travelling across America with a young girl in his passenger seat and then, I don't know, being abducted by aliens in the New Mexico desert; it may have been something like this that ultimately happened to Jim Sullivan, but we don't really know. Aliens, perhaps. The mafia, maybe. As for me, I don't know. And I don't know if one day we'll ever know. If one day someone on their deathbed will confess to a mafia hit, or even if a storm in the desert will reveal Jim's fossilized bones. I don't know.

Chapter 8

Jim Sullivan left San Diego, California one morning in March 1975. He kissed his wife and son, telling them that soon they would join him in Nashville, Tennessee, where he hoped his music would finally gain an audience.

Jim Sullivan never got to Nashville. He drove all day across Arizona before being pulled over by the New Mexico police at about seven in the evening because he was no longer driving straight. They took him to the police station to make sure he wasn't drunk. But Jim wasn't drunk, he was just very tired and was falling asleep at the wheel. So, they let him go and advised him to spend the night in Santa Rosa.

He took a room in a hotel called La Mesa. He paid the seventeen dollars in advance at the reception. He took his guitar and his bag from the trunk of his Volkswagen and put them in his room. A little later, he went to the liquor store to buy a bottle of vodka, but instead of going back up to his room to drink it, he got back in his car, drove a few miles along the back roads surrounding the town, and parked in the middle of nature, but not far from a home that looked like a ranch. This much we know because the owner later testified to the sheriff that he saw a car with its lights on, so he left his house and asked Jim if he had a problem. Jim replied: "No, do you?"

And after that, no one really knows what happened. Most likely, he restarted the car and drove about twenty-five miles into the desert, since it was about twenty-five miles from the village that they found his car. After which, we don't know. We know only that in the area there are more reports of extra-terrestrial phenomenon than anywhere else in the United States. And there you have it, that's America; no one knows what happened and his body was never found.

Part III

Chapter 1

In Warren, in front of the repair shop where Dwayne had bought his Dodge Coronet for the modest sum of six thousand dollars, next door to the diner where Milly continued to serve hamburgers and American coffee, you could browse the biggest video store in the city until ten o'clock. As it said on the banner hanging outside, the store had close to five thousand films for sale within a floor area of more than three thousand square feet. In winter when it got dark early, you could see the store from Van Dyke Avenue thanks to its flashing, electric blue tube lights that framed the logo and acted as a landmark of Michigan by night, from Monday to Saturday comforting the lonely souls whose only hope of an evening was to buy a case of beer at the corner store and rent an exciting action film. Something uncomplicated, they would ask Dwayne, lost in the middle of five thousand duds that seemed to taunt him and made him want to apologize when he took the customer's five-dollar bill. Five dollars for this shit, Dwayne would frequently think, lowering his gaze. Ronny Reagan had a standard response for such situations: "What do you think," Ronny said, "that supermarket cashiers have an opinion about what you put in your cart?"

From the very first day, Dwayne told himself that it couldn't last long, that life he had ended up agreeing to for Milly's sake; in other words, he swallowed his pride and started working in the video store, after Milly had a word with Ronny Reagan, who ate lunch at the same table almost every day and seemed to have a soft spot for her.

Sometimes, it must be said, he even put his arm around her waist when she brought him his coffee and clasped her really tightly. She had to jerk herself loose. So, she told herself that the Ronny in question couldn't refuse her what she asked, that it would be really good, right beside the diner. For Dwayne, yes, it would be really good.

Ronny Reagan tried really hard to explain things to Dwayne, about how a store is like a territory, he said, it looks after itself, you understand? You don't earn respect by apologizing. And Ronny Reagan, with his little goatee, his earring, and the lizard tattoo on his neck, returned to the smoky back of the store, beneath the buzzing neon. And if you're here, he added from the back, don't think it's thanks to me. You're only here because of Milly.

If you happen to find yourself at the other end of your existence, Dwayne told himself, then that's the exact spot I'm in. He continued to say this every morning. However, he also told himself that this morning, and not another, would be the last, and that soon he'd no longer see the parade of Michigan lumberjacks get their porn after having bought their cartons of cigarettes for the weekend hunting trip. Also, every day, as he ate at Milly's, he continued to imagine setting off down America's roads with her in the passenger seat, still wearing her black waitress's skirt because they would have left so fast; he imagined the miles as barbed wire that they would put between them and this Michigan, too dirty or too vulgar for her, he thought. Because it was true, those times on Van Dyke Avenue, the America of Sterling Heights, the America of white house fronts and university professors, were long, long gone

When Dwayne saw Ronny clasp her by the waist, when he saw her smiling at him, or even removing his arm with a firm hand, if by any chance Ronny's hand slid down over her butt, he told himself that maybe he was the one who had no business being there: watching Milly endlessly chew her gum, with her nametag on her chest and her hair that seemed more discolored in the neon lights. It's certain that this was a different Milly than the one who had lain her head on his stomach and talked to him about William Faulkner while smoking in the sunlight. And it's certain that at eighteen years old, you have more sides than at fifty. And it's certain too that he'd see another Milly soon, another of her sides.

I don't know if now is the right time to talk about this, but the fact is that if it ended between them, it was because of a side of her that he didn't know, that he never should have known, and perhaps which he never would have known had he followed Ronny Reagan's instructions. Meaning if he hadn't left the video store in the middle of the day to go to the repair shop on the other side of the street to talk about his old Dodge—the type of garage you only find in the United States, with American flags fluttering atop poles and a hundred used cars parked in no particular order, old metallic Thunderbirds and Lexuses resting on the battered cement, almost the way you might imagine a herd of bison on the Nebraska plains (the same sun at its zenith, the same tensed, immobile power of the herd, the same menacing fuselages). So, to return to Milly's sides, the shortest way to the repair shop was to go out past the video store's storage shack, a kind of small hangar with a sheet metal roof where Ronny stored old cassettes and cases. Exactly where he'd said he was going that afternoon to do a little tidying up.

Dwayne would have passed by as usual that day, without even turning his head, had he not heard a rather strange noise. It sounded like a sick animal, or something even more intriguing, something that made him want to slow his steps and put his ear to the door, and he quite quickly understood that there in storage, Ronny Reagan wasn't recycling the cassette cases. But as he opened the door, never would he have imagined that the first thing he would see, other than the three or four guys who stood waiting with folded arms, other than the video camera one of them held on his shoulder, never would he have imagined that the first thing he would see, under the thousand-watt spotlight, would be Milly's ass.

Even from behind he recognized Ronny Reagan, his on-edge silhouette as he told Milly that she should scream louder because they couldn't hear anything, while next to Milly there were two huge guys with erections, framing her, as it were. And Dwayne felt nothing. Neither hate nor desire nor sadness. Nothing. But he was rooted to the spot in the doorway of the shack that they had more or less turned into a mechanic's workshop—which is to say, they had converted into it a set for the movie, given that the two actors were playing the role of two mechanics in a garage.

The story was simple: a girl brings in her car to be repaired, the two mechanics are about to take care of it, but in order to not waste too much time, the scene entailed that she would thank them in advance. So, she started stroking the hood of her car, making innuendoes to the effect that the two mechanics should have a look under her hood too, and other such dialogue with dual meanings. And as she said all this, she was already undoing the zippers of their blue uniforms and grasping their respective penises. They started panting harder and harder, mechanically repeating, "yes, oh yes," as her mouth went from one penis to the other, faster and faster.

Chapter 2

THE DOCTORS TALKED about war-induced post-traumatic stress disorder when, at the base where he was stationed, Dwayne began smoking in secret and giving a nervous start whenever he heard a noise, exactly the same as the symptoms of Vietnam veterans are described. But Vietnam or not, everyone agreed: he shouldn't have reacted like that. He shouldn't have silently turned his back on Milly's ass or walked away so serenely, as if he had envisaged the scenario for months and was therefore mechanically enacting what ensued step by step, gesture by gesture.

He walked past the grubby diner windows. He crossed the parking lot and then Van Dyke Avenue at the crosswalk. He then entered the small store at the front of the service station. He headed to a section in the back to get a one-gallon gas can, he paid for it with a couple of bills he found at the bottom of his pocket, he walked towards pump number four, inserted the nozzle in the gas can, and filled it with gas.

With a slightly heavier tread, now that the gas can was full, he crossed back over the avenue, then the parking lot. Then he passed in front of the diner again and entered not the shack, not the set of the film that must still have been in progress, but the video store, a dozen feet further along, among the five thousand films that seemed to be waiting in the somber light of late evening.

He seemed to reflect for a moment on how to proceed; and then, still mechanically, he unscrewed the cap of the gas can, which he calmly placed on the cashier's desk. Next, he poured out the slightly syrupy, slightly smelly contents over every shelf of video cassette cases; the gas slowly trickled over the breasts of actresses and dripped to the floor, soaking into the carpet. He went around the whole store like that, evenly distributing the gas that soaked into everything up to the curtains, shaking the last drop out of the gas can before casually tossing it in the corner. Then going back to the cash register, he took the ten- and twenty-dollar bills that filled it, slipped them in his jean pockets, then opened the drawer below and removed the small book of complimentary matches emblazoned with the logo of a gun shop (two small crossed revolvers in a black circle against a yellow background). Next, he headed to the exit, coming to a stop in the doorway, where he lit a match, which he flicked into the middle of the store as a finishing touch.

The flame of the match traced an ornamental arc through the air before hitting the floor and multiplying itself a thousandfold, tracing lines of fire over the pink carpet and travelling the length of each aisle like an army of light, which by now had erased the actresses' faces, devouring them in the flames, engulfing every case before Dwayne's emotionless gaze. Now he turned, leaving to the heat he felt on his back the five thousand films whose smell of plastic would pervade the entire city for two days.

It's not for a lack of trying to imagine the conversation between Dwayne and Milly, which is to say, the one that would have taken place had he chosen the path most would have chosen: if he had left the shack, sat there in the diner, and waited for her. Seeing her come back, he would have said something like: "I need to talk to you." He would have let her sit down in front of him, lowered his eyes to focus on his glass of beer, and then started off with a sentence like "If you're doing it for money . . ."

But Milly, maybe out of pride or even because it was the truth, rather than saying something that would partly have erased his humiliation, would have looked him straight in the eye and told him that she didn't have to explain herself to an old soak, that she did what she wanted with her body and that he could fuck off. Obviously, the tone would then have grown heated and he wouldn't have been able to hold back, there in the diner where customers were eating, he wouldn't have been able to stop himself from saying things like "slut" or "whore," and that all she had going for her was to carry on getting screwed by that asshole Ronny Reagan.

But that conversation didn't take place, and deep down he didn't regret it, he didn't regret having put such a clear end to that part of his life, even though a few days later, in late summer 2001, he found himself in a psychiatric ward—influenced by the doctor's opinion, due to the alcohol, due to Vietnam, due to Milly, that was what the judges had ruled, they had deemed him to have acted out of insanity, that prison would destroy him further and that a stay in the psychiatric hospital would be more beneficial to him.

In my novel—given the concordance of the dates and given that I absolutely wanted to mention the event—it is also from the Northville Hospital room that Dwayne was able to see a Boeing 744 on the TV screen hanging from the wall as it plunged into one of the World Trade Center towers, at which, like millions of other Americans simultaneously, he said something like "Oh my God!" repeating it just like that, "Oh my God!" at least four or five times, and after that day, all the Americans' brains seemed to become enraged for a long time. In any case, it was enough for the doctors noticeably to increase the doses of Prozac, Naltrexone, and Xanax, as the head doctor was to explain to Susan—not Milly, but Susan, who remembered that she was the mother of his children and came to visit Dwayne, while Milly was still very angry.

And maybe it was better that way, thought Dwayne. Maybe when it came to a girl like Milly, she disappeared from a life the same way she entered it, which is to say, at the snap of a finger.

But with Susan, it was different. With you it's different, he'd tell her when she came to visit him. She'd sit down beside his bed, waiting for him to come back to them, to their Sterling Heights home. At least that's what Dwayne started to think. He felt better and better, he explained to Susan, that soon he'd be ready to lead a normal life, if you consider that there, at the heart of an asylum, you're not surrounded by normal life, if you consider that in his whole life Dwayne had yet to live a single normal day. But now that would change, now he realized a lot of things, and everything would start again from scratch: the children, Susan, and the university. Yes, everything would be like it was before.

Maybe he's actually better, said Susan in the doctor's office, maybe the Prozac isn't useless. But in the doctor's, as it were, glazed look, she understood that she shouldn't say things like that, not so soon. It was as if they were wrong about the length of his stay or about his idea of getting better, given that it took her a long time to relinquish the habit of counting the days and weeks, whereas the doctor, partly out of experience, partly out of resignation, always counted the years.

Moreover, he'll only get better, he added, slightly lowering his eyes, when he quits thinking that they shoot porno films in the hallways.

It was as if the doctor knew things that Dwayne didn't know about himself. Things that surely the doctor wouldn't tell Dwayne; but it was also as if everything already spoke volumes: his way of entering his office for the first time, the way he shook his hand, or his tone of voice when he said hello. And so, by shaking hands, the doctor could touch the wobbly beams of Dwayne's mind, and he could already predict that one day Dwayne would find himself once again in a Dearborn or Royal Oak bar. With his old friend Ralph, for example, underneath the red neon of a Budweiser sign, with slightly vintage music in the background, a Johnny Cash or Hank Williams sort of music—a slightly rock ambiance for people their age—bars that are deserted from Monday to Thursday but then are packed, without anyone really knowing where all the people come from, at around nine o'clock on a Saturday night.

And of course, the doctor was right. Of course, the day would arrive when Dwayne started drinking again. If it hadn't, a half-empty bottle of Jack

Daniels wouldn't have been sitting on the passenger seat of his Dodge Coronet just one year later. And of course it would have to be with Ralph, which is to say, Ralph would come looking for him when he finished his treatment and take him to a bar with red and blue neon lights at the edge of a major highway, on a Monday evening, for example, with a poorly lit pool table where two taciturn bikers were getting bored, with a slightly masculine, not very likeable waitress (a waitress much older than Milly, who would be called Daisy, since as far as I am concerned, in the United States, if a waitress isn't called Milly, she's called Daisy), a waitress who'd have nothing else to do that evening than dry the glasses and dust the shelves.

Both of them sat there at the bar, he and Ralph, discussing their lives. His now boring life in Sterling Heights, Ralph lamented, now that Dwayne was no longer there. Even more so now that he was retired, he added, which he hadn't imagined would be so difficult. He had spent thirty years crisscrossing the Mid-West to sell veterinary products—the rather melancholy kind of job that you find in American novels, although he might just as easily have been an executive in a waste recycling company or even a real estate agent in a rundown neighborhood.

If I were a real American novelist, I would certainly have taken the opportunity to delve into the details of Ralph Amberson's life, all the years he spent in Arkansas or South Dakota, because there, yes, it was the America in pain, the America of old rifles in the flat beds of pick-ups and John Deere trucks rusting in sheds, the America of Kansas cows by night and the Iowa grasshoppers that tear through wheat fields, not to mention all the solitary homes sitting out there in the plains, as if in front of the ocean, surrounded by tornadoes in the July heat.

If one day I go to the United States, what's for sure is that I won't go to the Mid-West or anywhere in middle America, because I'd have too much of an impression of having been swallowed by a whale, given that viewed from above on a globe, I find America resembles a whale. In any case, my idea of Americans like Ralph Amberson is that they spend the greater part of their lives sleeping in the belly of a whale, and that it's so dark in there that they're no longer capable of diving into their spouse's eyes when the time comes to retire. So, that was possibly what happened with Becky, or at least that was what Ralph confessed to Dwayne that evening, that he didn't look at her much any more. And that in the end, she gladly sought out other men. Ralph didn't have to be more explicit. He didn't have to mention the names that angered them both. He didn't mention Alex Dennis.

And for that matter, it would be Dwayne who did the talking that evening, going on and on, endlessly, about his last few years, enough to make it obvious that all of America really had turned its back on him, that he was going to end up like an old hobo on the West Coast, watching the boats leave San Francisco's port like his ancestors did the port of Amsterdam.

So of course, that day, there'd be a long moment's hesitation before he ordered a drink, with Dwayne saying something like, "Just speaking about it makes me want to drink something other than this shitty Diet Coke." And then there would be the half-understood silence that crossed his face, or rather the way he didn't look at Ralph right then. Then perhaps he would take the mental, the neurological journey that would produce the same phrases commanded by desire, or rather by need, in any case, something that medicine couldn't have completely stopped—such simple phrases that perhaps remained unsaid but which corresponded with expressions just as stupid as, "What can happen if I have just one drink?" or even, "Anyway, it's all I have left," and all the negotiations he made with his existence, his time on Earth, his future condition, before inevitably capitulating. One beer, then two, then a whiskey, please, Daisy; anyway, America has never been grateful to the Kosters, who have done more for America than the Senate and Congress. Be that as it may, they left the bar in a state of the utmost inebriation, took a room in a crummy motel, collapsed fully clothed on a bad mattress, before cursing themselves awake, full of inner dirtiness, so that they would be the only two who knew.

But as for abstinence, Dwayne already regretted, it had gone out the window. He admitted it while drinking some coffee, which turned his stomach, since he wasn't used to it, at least that was what turned his stomach that morning, but what nagged at him over the next few hours wasn't the alcohol, but certain things that Ralph Amberson had said the night before, things that he tried to remember in detail, that he felt were important; but what with the alcohol and the migraine clamping his head, he had a lot of trouble.

He remembered they had talked about Susan, about her moving away, about her new life in Rochester Hills. He remembered swearing he would go and see her, even that he would win her back. Dwayne said that after his fourth bourbon, yes, he would win her back, he insisted. And then Ralph, he also remembered, had begun talking about Roman emperors, yes, about Roman emperors; that he'd read somewhere that when they returned from a military campaign, or anyway the day before returning home, the Roman emperors always sent a messenger to announce their return. And in your opinion, Ralph asked, in your opinion, why did they do that? Well I don't know, Dwayne said, so that they would be given a magnificent welcome? No, Dwayne, they did that to be certain that they would find another man in their wife's bed.

Chapter 3

ADULTERY IS A very important part of American novels. It's even an obsession of American novels: the husband or the wife, even after divorce, has a history with someone else, and if possible, with the person that the other hates the most. I don't know whether we really grasp what Dwayne understood about those stories of emperors and their messengers; but what's certain is that henceforth he started to showing up in Rochester Hills on the gloomy evenings with which this story began, his car radio alternating between Jim Sullivan and the war in Iraq.

There, at the steering wheel of his Dodge, his fingers tensing a little more because of his taut nerves, his brain seeming to go round and round faster than the kids on their bikes, he thought again about those Roman emperors sending a message ahead. Dwayne thought that by parking there those last few weeks, he was, in a way, acting as his own messenger, that soon he'd inform the real Dwayne Koster of the situation, that soon he'd calmly explain the problem to him. Yes, the problem was named Alex Dennis. Yes, it was Alex Dennis behind the kitchen windows whom he saw kissing Susan like in a dark theater. By calmly telling himself that, things now made sense; yes, they slowly started to make sense.

It was at this moment, I wrote, that Dwayne Koster once more thought about Lee Matthews, about certain things he had said about having the power to make problems disappear, all the obscure things he had hinted at, about Dwayne bearing too heavy a burden and having to lighten it, about how he, Matthews, could lighten it.

It was this kind of thought that now lit up like an arc lamp in Dwayne's head, the type of thought that could drastically topple his existence from one moment to the next. He was both a fragile and a nervous man—especially now that he had started drinking again and also because he was now out of the doctor's claws, which had held him down for the past eighteen months, meaning the claws that kept him from being lucid about his situation. But now things are a lot clearer, yes, transparent, Dwayne Koster thought as the radio continued to broadcast the GIs' arrival on Iraqi soil: the night-vision goggles that lit the night green and grey on the world's screens, the planes catapulted into the Kuwaiti sky.

And Jim Sullivan seemed to appear, superimposed on his windshield, telling him not to get annoyed. Don't get worked up, Dwayne, said Jim Sullivan.

Part IV

Chapter 1

That Lee Matthews was an international art trafficker, that Dwayne Koster ended up in Lee's shady orbit, I never doubted, or that the reader would be able to understand all of that long before I clearly laid it out in the continuation of my book. And when he parked his Dodge at the top of Clark Street, when he calmly greeted Lee Matthews in his shop in Chicago, there was no doubt in anyone's mind that at that very moment, Dwayne had finally stepped into a minefield. And it was so much clearer than it was during the whole scene: when Lee welcomed Dwayne and apologized for not coming to see him at the clinic—not once, Dwayne said, you didn't come even once, he even emphasized—as he calmly led him into the back of his store. You could see very well that, apart from two or three browsers minutely examining the flaws of an old Chinese vase, there was a lone man, oddly alone, who was way more interested in their interaction than in the antiques.

It's even through his eyes that we might best understand the unfolding action, rather like the traveling shot that you would use to follow Lee as he discretely led Dwayne into the backroom that clearly served as his office. It's even through his ears that we might hear Lee's voice telling Dwayne that he was going to take care of his little problem.

But in return, said Lee, you'll have to do me a little favor. And Dwayne, despite furrowing his brow and breathing nervously, replied: Yes, of course, anything that you want, Lee.

Then out of precaution or reflex, Lee closed the door to his office so that no matter how loudly he spoke, the lone man roaming around the shop wouldn't hear anything but a continuous murmur, from which words like "Iraq", "dollars", then "shipment", and also "Baltimore" stood out, but among which phrases like "I'll take care of Alex" or "We're totally agreed then" remained unclear, till suddenly we no longer hear anything else that is being said. Of course, the conversation continues, but the volume becomes muted, after which the lone man doesn't hear the rest—and neither do we, since we were depending on him to hear what they were saying. What's certain is that it was several minutes before both of them reappeared amongst the browsers, who hadn't moved. In Dwayne's hand there was now a leather briefcase, which, from the way he was holding it, we could clearly see wasn't his. Which is to say, we could clearly see the tangled web of thoughts that were being woven in his brain and which, as it were, transported him to another world, a world exotic and certainly dangerous.

At least this is what the lone man, who continued to listen from a distance, thought he heard from Lee Matthews's mouth, something like: "If you end up in the shit, no one's going to pull you out." Yes, the lone, intriguing man had heard that perfectly, and took good note.

And surely, if we'd followed the man in question earlier, we'd have understood a lot of things when it comes to Lee Matthews, given that this lone, intriguing man who observed everything was really an FBI agent and had been investigating Matthews for some time—the type of man whom in another scene of my book we saw speak to his superior and explain the situation to him, saying things like "yep" and "I think this whole business goes all the way to the top," which allowed us to gain an inkling of what was going on. For example, the complicated connections between Lee Matthews and the Iraq War, and a thousand other things invisible to the naked eye, but which the FBI guy had good reasons to suspect. Things that didn't directly concern Dwayne Koster, but unfortunately, they also did to some extent.

Chapter 2

April 5, 2003, 01:00 GMT, the American army stationed in Kuwait decided to terminate the Iraqi regime. Restless tanks whose tracks compacted the sand under the weight of their slow advance shot blindly at anything they thought they saw moving. The journalist said on the radio that in the Iraqi plain and the Baghdad suburbs, there was something moving everywhere they looked: a dog, a man, or even a tissue blowing in the wind. They shot more or less as rapidly as their pounding heartbeats, overly-armed soldiers who jumped out of their trucks screaming and acting like a hailstorm descending on the cities of Falluja and Baghdad. The children, the women, and the men were already hidden at the back of the labyrinth, concealing themselves from the soldiers' screams, the journalist continued, enveloped in a mist of tear gas. Via the thousands of videos posted so quickly on the internet, it became a type of urban Vietnam, where the enemy, if there even was one, was invisible, would pop up unexpectedly in the middle of four or five G.I.'s, who would scream the words heard in a thousand war films: "shit" and "fuck" and "get out of here!" before the shredded body of the one who had jumped on the bomb or received the stab wound in the last burst reassured his comrades, telling them yet again, "I'm not going to die here," while his cell phone, fallen to the ground, recorded nothing more than the cloudy sky which seemed already to have welcomed the placated spirits, the soldier and his murderer now reconciled in death.

While chaos ruled the city, groups of looters showed up everywhere: in the ministries, the marble palaces, and the national museum where for almost one hundred years the vestiges of Sumer and Babylon had rested. The Fedayeen looted the items of the museum's collections by the dozens, each returning to his home with an artefact of their extremely old history. One a vase, another a necklace, another a small statue representing a god unearthed by the archeologists.

And everywhere, on the TV, in the newspapers, we heard the same outraged words, that the soldiers posted there had done nothing, and that also, to tell the truth, those Arabs didn't have any respect for anything.

But scarcely days after the sacking of the city,

the newspapers all around the world changed their tune and suspected a conspiracy, that the pillaging of Baghdad's national museum and the priceless Sumerian collections was not the actions of a popular uprising or even the citizens acting like bandits, but was a more organized operation, planned by international traffickers. We're talking about some four thousand pieces methodically hidden—methodically, yes, that's how the media at the time began describing it, reporting the curator's testimony that the thieves didn't seem to be simple Fedayeen, but were highly organized men who, surprise, surprise, had left behind all the copies and painstakingly taken all the originals.

Some people said that the American army let it happen. Some people said that soldiers were paid not to intervene. Some said that the fencing of the items was carefully planned and most of the pieces had ended up in the homes of collectors. What's certain is that some profited from the traffic, that by now, against the backdrop of Iraqi shops, beneath neon lights darkened by thousands of gnats and the smoke of Marlboros, telephones were ringing non-stop as the prices of the pieces were negotiated ready for them to be shipped to the other side of the Atlantic, to the docks of New York and Baltimore. By now they were getting ready to receive the merchandise, under the lethargic eye of customs officers who knew, who knew with mathematical precision, that in the two thousand or so containers which they swept with a single glance there were millions of items of illicit merchandise—drugs of course, weapons certainly, but also an old Sumerian vase, or even fragments of a statue representing Hammurabi or Gilgamesh. Whichever of the two, they were pieces directly imported from Iraq in the spring of 2003, ready to travel another thousand miles to be put in a museum or even an antique dealer's store, if possible, an antique dealer with connections to my story.

In fact, you didn't need to be psychic to understand that Lee Matthews was involved in this affair. This was precisely why he had entrusted a briefcase full of money to his nephew—300,000, Lee told Dwayne, the briefcase contains more than 300,000 dollars in new notes, so I advise you not to let them flutter away like dead leaves. Once more, the FBI agent heard him, and he began to put together all the pieces of the puzzle.

Little by little, the FBI agent realized that the puzzle in question had a lot of pieces due to all the things that we missed out on afterwards, notably that the whole trafficking affair implicated highly placed people from the region—General Motors executives, big Republican Party donors—just as it was discovered that a part of the profits would serve to finance the campaign of a future governor, and other such absolutely eye-opening things.

Among other things it was discovered that a large

part of the funds was intended for Illinois, because in Illinois, according to the information collected by the agent, there was a guy from the Democratic Party who had seriously begun to bother them, although little did anyone know at that point, in 2003, that the guy in question would become the first black president of America.

Chapter 3

I DIDN'T STRESS the point in my novel, because I didn't want to turn it into a political thriller with complicated stories that mix together real-life people and fictional characters, the way American authors often do, it's true. After all, even if I was constantly looking toward America in my work, I was still a French author. It's not customary for the French to mix together real people and fictional characters. That's why I didn't mention Barrack Obama's name in my novel. That's why I didn't say that Dwayne Koster nonetheless held a part of America's fate in his hands, even if that's why the FBI agent wouldn't let him out of his sight until the transaction took place, because the FBI agent had indeed deduced that there would be a transaction.

Dwayne still had to travel the seven hundred miles to Baltimore, because that's where the transaction was to take place, although, true, Dwayne could still drop out.

One hundred times that day, after laying the briefcase flat in the trunk, one hundred times he almost dropped out, because he could easily have thrown the briefcase off a bridge, or even have started his life anew with it. He too dwelled on it hundreds of times: why not change your name and go to Hawaii, or deepest Vermont? Anywhere so long as he disappeared, he thought again on the six-lane Columbus highway, hesitating to turn off for Cincinnati or Lexington. Because it was 300,000 dollars . . . 300,000 dollars, he repeated, as if that was the exact sum that would have cushioned his fall, as if all at once he'd forgotten about the real America, the America he'd dreamed about all these years, in all those books he'd read, the dusty America on the shelves of his Ann Arbor office—the America that was the exact opposite of money. It was the exact opposite of a full briefcase in a trunk, the possibility of living on nothing other than the fortune made by life itself; Thoreau said so, Whitman said so, Emerson said so, and Dwayne thought so too that evening as he turned off the engine in a motel parking lot in the suburbs of Baltimore.

In the room at the Motor Inn that he'd ended up renting—I wrote—the same as every time he entered a motel, Dwayne Koster thought about Jim Sullivan. He placed the briefcase on the fluffy bedspread. Then he turned on the sad ceiling light that illuminated the entire room, the poster of dolphins above the bed, the red lamp on the nightstand. And then he sat there in the only armchair in the sixty-square-foot room, watching the briefcase as if it were a screen or a book that might have told the future, as if it were a set of colors or pictograms that might have told him what to do. Continuing to stare like a curious animal, he asked himself whether or not he should take it to dinner with him. It would be odd to take it to dinner with him, but he didn't trust the Pakistanis at reception; either way, he'd feel nervous no matter what.

At around ten p.m., he was back in his room. He would have liked to draw the blinds, but there weren't any. He thought about Susan. Also, about Alex Dennis. And he thought again about Lee, about the conversation he'd had with Lee. Dwayne had made it clear that he shouldn't be too hard on him, just teach him a little lesson, enough to get him away from Susan once and for all. Of course, Lee had said, don't worry, they'll do it gently.

A little later, Dwayne watched surprising things on the TV: tractor races, documentaries on pike fishing, a plastic surgery operation. And then there were the channels he didn't check out. He was too afraid. What if he chanced to see Milly . . . Milly's butt . . . No. He'd better not. He thought again about the way she'd uttered the name "William Faulkner" in motel bedrooms, about how she'd gazed outside with the white, milky sky reflected in her eyes, about how she was so confident in front of the mirror in the bathroom.

Around midnight, he still was at the window, smoking. Maybe he should have seen the guy from behind. Maybe he should have realized that he'd seen him somewhere before. But he didn't pay any attention. And at the same time that was the goal, that the guy in question remain incognito in Dwayne's eyes despite having taken the same highways, despite having crossed the same monotonous plains under the same mackerel skies. That was the goal: continue to follow him and observe him with impunity, at least until Dwayne carried out his instructions, the briefcase gripped tighter and tighter in his hand, more and more magnetized by the exchange that was more and more imminent.

At least that's what the FBI agent recorded as he pushed aside the branches of a tree to aim his telephoto lens at Dwayne Koster and observed him enter a park that overlooked the bay, briefcase in hand: tomorrow, Baltimore docks. Dwayne was no longer afraid, hypnotized by the path he had to take, mechanically pushing open the little gate of the children's playground before sitting on a bench from which he first brushed the flower petals, sitting and waiting because he had a meeting.

And barely a few minutes after Dwayne sat down, a few minutes after he placed his briefcase beside him, the agent observed two rather bearded men come and sit down on the bench next to his. They were clearly Arabs, clearly large, made even larger by the long djellabas that came to below their knees, and they seemed to be making small talk, watching as their kids played in the sandbox.

You can easily be an Iraqi activist, finance the war against America by selling your nation's heritage, and have kids. The same as you can easily be an American, abandon your kids along with your wife, and give a briefcase full of money to said Iraqis so that they can arm themselves against your own compatriots. That's what Dwayne himself was about to do, sitting there on a bench and looking out to sea. Watching the kids in the playground, feeling sorry for little Samira because her father had forcibly planted her in the middle of the sandbox, perhaps Dwayne even wondered for a second if one day he'd see his own kids again.

And Lee Matthew's words came back to him, "Be careful, Dwayne. No one will cover you if you do something stupid . . . no one." But Dwayne was no longer really himself for him still to be afraid, something wasn't quite there, as if it had evaporated into thin air.

Then one of the two Arabs got up. He walked over to his daughter, who'd swallowed some sand, or who for some other reason had started crying, spitting and coughing up whatever she could. As if concerned, Dwayne also stood up, as if by accident leaving the briefcase on the bench, and approached the sandbox. He took his turn consoling the girl all while staring at the father's long fingers as he traced several letters in the damp sand where Samira was crying—he did so like an old sage in the Moroccan desert, one might have said—but the FBI agent thought, yes, that's obviously how they're exchanging information, for example, the name of the cargo ship that's going unload this evening at dock number three.

And it was obvious that Dwayne wasn't going to collect the merchandise there, in a children's park—although at this point in the story we don't yet know exactly what it was, only that it was antiques and worth a fortune, also only that the next part happened near the dock whose number one of the Arabs had just erased from the surface of the sand with a swipe of his foot, because they were professionals and because the stakes were high. They were particularly high if you consider that with the 300,000 dollars in the briefcase the Iraqis could buy themselves some M16s from Pakistan and keep flipping fuel trucks in the desert; also if you consider that once the operation was completed, Dwayne Koster wouldn't have to hear about Alex Dennis any more.

Chapter 4

Surely, if someone had observed the guys hired by Lee, both of them hopping on the same large motorcycle, adjusting the black visors of their helmets in the silence that submerged their departure—the silence so quickly broken by the abrupt sound of the engine, then the thrum of acceleration—surely, if someone had seen them, they would quickly have understood that given the faceless toughness of their full helmets, they needed to be stopped right away.

Because surely it didn't take much imagination to understand what kind of guys we were dealing with, the kind that voluntarily complete their part (no, maybe not voluntarily, but let's say without too much hesitation, in any case, not enough for them to give up or to fail) of what we call a contract, meaning the summary execution of a nuisance, arranged for a sum of money that pretty much everyone can take out of their wallet—sometimes even for a lot less—to buy the service and silence for said service.

Except that this time, all the same, it wasn't exactly that. That evening, you would have said that the motorcycle was a mode of transport like any other when they wisely parked it outside a bar somewhere between Trenton and Monroe, since they had decided to grab a drink, as we would also wisely have assumed. And entering straight away, they sat down at the bar and ordered a beer for the one and a whiskey for the other, placidly watching a barroom that wasn't very busy on that night of the week. And so, we wouldn't have suspected that they were there for any other reason.

Except that among the few people dancing or talking or getting bored on the couch, there was one that interested them. They even knew they'd find him there at that time, at eleven-thirty p.m. or midnight; to be honest, they'd made the trip especially for him that evening and had no problem recognizing him, because they knew him. But not the other way around. He didn't know them. So, he wasn't worried.

For that matter, they didn't walk over to interrupt the conversation he'd struck up with a girl younger than he was, about an electric blue cocktail that we might without error conclude was made with curaçao, milk, ice, and, as ordered by the two drinking from the same glass, two straws. She was a girl for one or two nights, since Alex Dennis was also known for his tendency to seduce young woman, his reputation for making their heads spin.

But it's also certain that that evening, if there are verbs to place in the imperfect tense, then they are those to do with his intention to seduce. And it's also certain that at the very moment I say this, all eyes turn toward the bar where the two bikers are still sitting, seemingly unrushed and uninterested in knowing whether the blue cocktail couple are going to order something else or even whether he's going to stand up, pay, then leave, and so, it's certain he's going to take her home with him. The two know that he won't take her home.

That evening, they're going to walk out the door of the bar rather quickly, hand in hand, they're going to have time to go over to his car, time for her to sit down in the passenger seat. Next, it's certain that he won't have time to wear out his masculine powers since the second he walked around the back of his large GMC to reach the driver's seat on the other side, the aforementioned bikers, one on each side, escorted him into the night, so unobtrusively that the anonymous girl still waiting for him didn't turn around right away. They took him under some trees, one of them held his hand over his mouth while the other made sure that Alex Dennis understood that you don't do certain things.

Then he lost consciousness, barely hearing one

of the guys say, as they gazed down at him on the ground, something like: "This is for everyone in Michigan who's been cheated on." And then the time came for the girl to grow suddenly alarmed, to call out Alex's name several times, turning toward the bar where the bouncer had no doubt understood what happened (not in detail, no, but he understood, let's say, that certain things end up paying for themselves). Then the police arrived, then the ambulance, and maybe the worst thing for him was the siren as they took him to the hospital, the siren that seemed to broadcast to the whole city that he'd lost his virility, and the fingers pointed at him by the gawkers who, you may well believe it, just as quickly forgot about this story and its protagonist.

Chapter 5

All ports are said to resemble one another. The same boats sag in the water under the weight of their containers. The same lichens attach themselves to the large rusty rings. The tidal range that can be gauged by the length of the seaweed against the jetty walls. The rust tones. Also, the feeling that nothing is ever new, that rust bathes the air in color, and, like tetanus, spreads over the docks at dusk.

In the end, we might have wondered if Dwayne Koster was about to fall asleep there on the shore of the Atlantic; so much time went by, so much time spent waiting, that everything seemed to crumble—especially the sense of things and the curve of time—so much so that falling night seemed also to descend on his whiskey-soaked soul.

It was only when he saw the beam of a flashlight directed at him from over the water that he remembered he wasn't there by accident, no, not at all by accident. He sat up straight in his seat and flashed his headlights toward Chesapeake Bay. Then, as if responding to the code clearly established between them, in the almost total darkness he saw the shadow of a boat detach itself little by little from the larger shadow of the cargo vessel, coming closer and closer to the dock, with its motor shut off, at which Dwayne got out of his car and prepared to meet them, pointing a flashlight at the ground, and the fear, obviously, the fear returned along with the night, causing him constantly to look behind him, to be alert to the slightest sound, because of the feeling that someone who shouldn't be there was positioned somewhere in the background of the port. And Dwayne reasoned with himself and told himself he was mistaken. And for a long time we thought that was true.

Do things in order, he tried to think, that's the most reasonable thing, he continued, his logic momentarily calming him, he told himself that afterward he would never again get involved in anything like that, that he wasn't the type for that kind of thing, that suddenly he'd start thinking that even Alex Dennis, right, he's a bad guy, right, he likes women, and he's ambitious, right, but does he deserve what they're going to do to him? What he didn't know was that it had already been done.

The silent boat neared the shore, and he took the mooring line. He moved smoothly and almost agilely despite the booze inside him. And he knew that none of the three silhouettes that disembarked would check his breath. Other than saying a few words that were also lost in the darkness, they unloaded several little wooden crates, three to be exact, placing them as quickly as possible in Dwayne's outstretched arms. He put them just as quickly in his trunk, right beside the hockey stick.

I haven't yet said what was in the crates, but they included some of the most priceless pieces from Baghdad's museum, pieces that witnessed the dawn of civilizations and which, in my book, had a symbolic value. Their value was great enough for me to be able to hope that the reader would pick up on it, since they included some of the oldest traces of writing ever to have been found in the world: the first stone tablets engraved with fragments of a Sumerian epic. Passages from the same epic were already on display in London and Paris, Lee Matthews explained to Dwayne—in fact before becoming a genuine criminal, Lee Matthews had actually been a specialist in the subject. Except that now, specialist or not, there were people ready to pay a good million dollars for those highly precious fragments. And as he wedged them in his trunk to keep them from moving, Dwayne remembered that at one point he himself had been a professor of literature. And Dwayne remembered Herman Melville and William Faulkner.

And once again Dwayne thought he heard noises, but he had been hearing noises for the last thirty years, so there was no reason that this time they would be more real than usual. And then he carefully, very carefully, closed the trunk of the Dodge. And carefully, very carefully, he sat behind the wheel, while on the water, faintly lit by the moon, he made out the three silhouettes of the men moving farther and farther from the shore, the boat's motor still shut off, their plashing oars the only sound. Dwayne turned, leaving the waterfront behind, climbed the slope above the port, and, told himself that with smooth rolling, he'd be able to deliver the precious tablets to his boss by tomorrow afternoon.

Chapter 6

HE HEARD NOISES anyway.

On the gloomy roads that fanned out across the country—I wrote—Dwayne Koster felt glued to his rearview mirror, since for more than an hour, on the four-lane highway that crossed Fort Wayne, it was obvious a car had been following him. And Dwayne had every reason not to feel comfortable at night on an American highway closed off by large trees on either side, with three crates of Iraqi antiquities in his trunk and the plausible suspicion that someone was out to get him.

He didn't mess around opening the crates of fragments that rattled around whenever he tapped the brakes, as if to remind him they were there. Rather, what he tried to do was to go over things in his mind, to summon any remaining lucidity in order to reflect, to know whether it was at least possible that someone might be following him, given all the precautions he'd taken: the detours in the night, avoiding lights when leaving cities, and losing himself, half-asleep, under the trees that border the major highways—the same trees that seemed to emerge from the headlights. We might have said that they woke up with a start to look at his car and tell him, like in the darkness of a fairy tale: stop, Dwayne, stop.

A bag of nerves, driving across Indiana, one eye on the rearview mirror, one on the road being swallowed under the long hood of his muscle car, he didn't like seeing the headlights reappear in the mirror after going around a curve. And Dwayne would accelerate, or brake, or do nothing, because at first, he didn't really want to know if someone was following him. He preferred not to think about the fact that the headlights behind him always kept practically the same distance, that they was like two eyes in the night, always fixated on him, in the rectangular sheen of the rearview mirror. And he barely remembered where he was going. To Detroit, of course. No, to Chicago, to see Lee Matthews. He had to give him the merchandise. Then they'd be square. He'd see Susan again. Or Milly. He didn't know any more. He could no longer figure out why he was returning to that humid, rusty region, those strips of earth that alternate with the surfaces of lakes. He'd be better off anywhere else, he thought, hunting mountain lions in Colorado or even in snowy

Wyoming, writing his own great American novel.

Little by little, panic overwhelmed him. And little by little he felt that the whole business no longer concerned him. So, it was time to decide. It was time to know for sure; so, he stopped at the next rest stop, and if the car behind him stopped as well, then he would see and think about making a second decision.

The other car stopped as well. And Dwayne saw it in the rearview mirror. He saw it slow down and stop in the pitch dark. And Dwayne sat there, still looking in his rearview mirror at the menacing headlights of the car parked three hundred feet behind him. Dwayne thought about, or rather turned over in his mind, his old combat training reflexes and the urge to enter the fray, as if at that Indiana highway rest stop he were back in Vietnam, in the mangrove swamp of a silty river. Except that instead of a silty river, it was the six lanes of Route 30, where tractor-trailers set the rhythm of the flow.

He opened his door and tried to act as if he hadn't seen the man back there in the concealing night. The door of the other car opened and the guy got out. There could be no doubt he was approaching Dwayne. Be that as it may, there was no doubt in his mind as he opened the trunk of his Dodge. He acted as if he was rummaging for something without really knowing what he was searching for. Anyway, it was too late to get rid of the crates, the ancient fragments he would have liked to toss down the john. Meanwhile from inside the car, Jim Sullivan's lyrics continued to waft—lyrics that I picked specifically for this occasion, which spoke of highways and solitude and lost identity, lyrics that Dwayne was no longer really listening to.

What he was listening to right then was the man's footsteps, which were audible on the asphalt: he was the type of guy who made the faux pas of putting metal toe plates on his shoes, which resounded throughout the parking lot, as if it seemed normal to him to be making so much noise. What I mean is that psychology has nothing to do with fear or tension, but on the contrary, it mimics calm people who are used to it. And it's certain, Dwayne thought, that it's easier to be calm when you have a P38 in your pocket. Dwayne thought, or imagined, that the barrel was already pointed at him, not to shoot, not even to make an impression, but just to get closer and closer still while Dwayne dared not to look, still absorbed in his trunk among the objects that occupied the space, amid the souvenirs of his previous life: Thoreau's name on the cover of *Walden*, the hockey stick, and Iggy Pop's face, which looked at him in such a brotherly way.

And suddenly, he no longer heard the sound of metal toe plates pounding on the ground. Suddenly, he knew that now he'd be able to hear the guy or see his shadow, to hear his breathing, or even more than his breathing, the sentence he was about to say, and that it would be something in the form of an understatement, something like: "Can I help you?" or "It's not very hot out for May."

But the words he almost spoke were unimportant since he failed to say them. Among the things in his trunk, Dwayne was by now firmly grasping the hockey stick, which he clutched like a child afraid that someone was going to steal his toy, his fingers as tensed as an eagle about to seize its prey. As the shoes had abruptly fallen silent, as he knew that at least three feet behind him there was a silhouette that didn't wish him well, in one movement Dwayne raised the hockey stick to shoulder height, as high as a golf club poised for a long drive. But instead of a golf ball, the stick hit the guy straight in ribs, and he collapsed just as quickly under the force of the blow. Rather than swinging just once, Dwayne struck the pose of an amateur golfer once more and hit him three times on the legs, on the back. He hit him hard, stopping himself before he caved the guy's skull in—meaning Dwayne suddenly regained a bit of awareness and, stick in the air, stopped in mid-swing, thought about what he was in the process of doing. Without knowing if the sudden cessation of the act was because of what he'd just done or even what he was about to do—in other words, incapable of knowing whether he'd gone too far or not far enough—as if in that small lapse of time something like the law had stepped between him and the man on the ground. Something like a penal code suddenly erected a wall before him, a wall that he tried to climb, at least to see what was on the other side; all those years without light in a prison cell, all those years that he would have to multiply by at least three or four when he saw the guy's badge, at the bottom of which the letters F, B, and I glinted in the night.

Chapter 7

WINTER WAS NOW completely gone. The cherry trees were now budding along the long avenues past Eight Mile Road. The smell of acacias now drifted through the partly opened window of the Dodge. He wouldn't have known how to explain why he had gone back there. It was the last thing he would have thought of doing had anybody asked him. Had someone said to him: Dwayne, what do you plan on doing now? On the highway in the middle of the night, the first thing he did was take out his phone and call Lee Matthews, and, screaming and gesticulating at the wheel, he told him that he'd messed up. I messed up, he said, and tears filled his eyes, like a lowly minion who begs forgiveness from his boss but will receive neither absolution nor protection. That very moment, at the other end of the line, all he heard was Lee's voice say, "No one will protect you, Dwayne. Not from something like this." At which point the phone was hung up on him, the disconnect tone leaving him astounded. Then Dwayne said to himself that if that's the way it is, Uncle Lee, then I swear you'll never see your tablets again.

By now he'd even forgotten about the restraining order. He was parked on the white paving stones of the driveway. It was late, and Susan was sleeping.

But sometimes it happens that even in the deepest sleep you sense something is awry. Susan will never know what dream or lack thereof made her blink open her eyes at eleven thirty p.m., according to the LCD screen of her alarm clock, and she had a very strange feeling that she had to get up, go to the window, to look out into the night and see whether it was the moon that dissipated the darkness. Except that instead of the moon, what she saw that night, lighting up the darkness, was the beam of a flashlight sweeping the ground and the roots of the trees, whitening the trunks with its block of glare.

The flashlight was pointed at the toolshed, and she saw a hand, or rather a glove encasing a hand, which turned the door handle. It didn't take her long to realize it wasn't a stranger sneaking around her garden at night, but none other than Dwayne Koster. If, that is, we can say it was the same Dwayne Koster whom she'd married twenty years earlier, I mean, the one she had kissed amid the roar of Niagara Falls—yes, she had that vision of them doubled up with laughter in the mist of the falls.

He rummaged through the shed quietly enough for her to understand that no one was supposed to hear him. The light pointed at the ground flaring out toward the interior. And then she saw a long wooden stick in his hand, like a shovel or pitchfork handle, and he went toward a spot behind the apple trees, the kind of spot where she went maybe twice a year to do some yard work.

She didn't need to see the tool distinctly to know it was definitely a shovel. She needed only to see the curve of his back in order to recognize the movements of a man digging a hole at night, his silhouette showing slightly different shades of black in the darkness. The silhouette didn't dance but made coordinated, calm, methodic movements. All she could hear was him panting from time to time, because he worked quickly. Just as quickly, he deposited in the hole the three wooden crates that had been taking up too much space in his trunk.

Susan saw everything in detail because she was still at her window and had no intention of moving, and certainly no intention of going back to sleep, because she wouldn't have been able to. So, she thought she was fine there: neither helping him nor making a move, but remaining where the two things were still possible and kept her from making a decision. That would have been the worst thing for her right then: to make a decision.

So, she watched him dig and refill the hole to

perfection—this she was able say with certainty, since the next day, when she inevitably went to take a look, there was nothing to see, not even a hole. She would have dug it up again herself had she not seen an FBI agent on the TV news that morning, who announced that a dangerous individual, armed with a hockey stick that he kept in his trunk, was missing along with fragments of a Sumerian epic.

And sure, he could have hidden them in a thousand places. He could have hidden them at the base of a tree or in one of the many lakes. He could have made a map and counted the number of paces in the direction of the rising sun. But no, he wouldn't have known how to explain why. Maybe he acted like cats, which bring their prey back to their master's home, thought Susan. He thought that the place for the Sumerian kings was in a garden in Michigan, a noble, secret sepulture where no one would ever disturb them. In any event, not Susan, it was true, she'd never say a thing. Maybe because she still loved Dwayne. Yes, maybe, she even thought so herself as he stowed the shovel in the shed and went back to his car without even looking up at her, at the window of her room, where maybe he would have caught a glimpse of her in the nearly black grayness.

No, he wouldn't have seen her. I mean, even in the middle of the day he wouldn't have seen her; because by now he understood that he belonged to an endless night . . . an American night, in a sense.

Right. After which, Dwayne Koster didn't hang around. He got moving again, without looking back and without really thinking. You might say that everything that occurred henceforth was beyond his brain or the vocabulary of his brain. You might say that the outside world was no longer reflected in the words he might have uttered, and he merely drove in the direction his car was pointing, remembering that just an hour before he'd beaten up a guy from the FBI, that because of that, he'd have all the country's police on his tail before dawn, but that also before dawn, he knew he'd be long gone.

Knowing that, he slowed down for a moment on Van Dyke Avenue. That's how we know he was trying to see Milly Hartway's silhouette through the bay windows of the diner.

Milly was indeed there, chewing gum as ever, vacuuming before closing time. And over there, at the booth near the windows, there was that imbecile Ronny Reagan seated with a huge hamburger, watching her, thought Dwayne, or maybe waiting for her. And of course, it was still the same Milly Hartway, with ankle tattoos and hair that had faded almost to white from being dyed, but for Dwayne, as he looked at her from the window of his car, for Dwayne she was no longer the student who had smiled at him in his Ann Arbor office, or even the naked girl he'd seen bathing in the June sun. No, for Dwayne, as he watched her vacuuming the floor,

Milly Hartway was like a stranger whose breasts and butt he would have been incapable of picturing.

So, he didn't turn into the parking lot. He didn't get out of his car. He didn't look her in the eye and tell her: "I'm leaving."

I hesitated on this point: he enters, takes a seat at the bar, and maybe asks her to go with him. I hesitated and then I told myself no, that didn't make sense. In America, the lines are drawn straight, they never go in circles.

And Dwayne turned his head away, looked straight ahead, at Van Dyke Avenue, and sped up. He even had the feeling that his 120-horse-power Dodge backed him up and told him to step on it. Step on it, Dwayne Koster, don't look back.

Then little by little, his insanity adapted to the landscape. Little by little the Dodge traced an invisible line, sliding through the breaking day, running along the Missouri roads and over the St. Louis Bridge, the same exhausted Dodge, tearing through America. You might say that it was endowed with a mind of its own, that it made Dwayne's decisions for him, and it didn't stop, as if diffracting the day from the time that belonging to it.

Now, there was nothing but silent countryside and sluggish wind, where only the prairie grass recalled the gusts of air left by the tractor trailers, where even the highway was scorched by a sun that the absence of trees along Route 44 all too little quelled. Even the highway seemed less hostile now, as if the waning day had released it from exhausting hours of combat, the metallic, throbbing combat in which Dwayne's car was engaged as it hurtled toward New Mexico. For there you have it, as has been clear for a long time: the reason for this book is Jim Sullivan.

Chapter 8

Dwayne Koster arrived in Santa Rosa one evening in May 2003. He took a room at the La Mesa Motel. He paid the forty dollars in advance at reception. He took his suitcase out of the trunk of his Dodge and he left it in his room. A little later, he ate dinner: a hamburger with fries and a large beer. A little later still, he went to bed.

At dawn, Dwayne woke up. He calmly placed his hand on the door handle and then left. He heard a coyote barking in the distance, but that had no effect on him. It was hot despite the early hour. He saw a few lizards dash across the sand and maybe even a snake, but neither had any effect on him. He climbed into his Dodge and drove a few miles down Interstate 80, then swung right onto Route 54, heading for El Paso. On the radio, he heard things that had to do with him, a wanted notice that more or less accurately described him. It described his car, now off-white from the two thousand miles he had traveled in three days. But it didn't have any effect on him. And Dwayne inserted the Jim Sullivan disc in the car's CD player. And he told himself that soon, yes, soon he'd be there, in the cracked desert.

Deep down inside, did he already know that he was going to end it? No, it's not possible, obviously, a person can't just sit behind the wheel of a car and consciously say to himself that he's going to end it. Let's say that one thought inside him, just one thought inside him, out of fifty possible thoughts, tends in that direction. He has fifty thoughts behind the wheel of his white Dodge Coronet, and out of all of those thoughts, he'll choose the one where he's going to end up in a ditch, where he'll jerk the steering wheel and veer into a ditch. No, of course not, he doesn't consciously tell himself that.

On the contrary, he consciously gets behind the wheel and concentrates, he gradually accelerates, very gradually, and he tells himself that it's all just like normal, a car that brakes and accelerates like normal. And in some ways, it's true. The car accelerates and brakes like normal, propelled from behind by one hundred twenty horses. Just like normal, he tells himself; but when he begins to think about it, he also tells himself he's screwed, because right then it's as if he really were being followed by a raging herd that tells him that he doesn't get to decide, but they do, the one hundred twenty horses, the one hundred twenty thoroughbreds galloping right behind him.

At least in his head that's what happened. That morning, his head thudded strangely, as if the thoroughbreds behind him had caught up with him, as if they were about to gallop over him. He really felt as if he had to accelerate down that straight road because they were about to gallop over him, trample him, and the more he accelerated, the more enraged they became, right behind him. He tried to tell himself things, he tried to tell himself that he should slow down a little; but the other one inside him, who was doing the driving, didn't respond. He didn't even know if he was listening right then, as all he could hear were the enraged horses right behind him, which trampled his brain. And then, I don't know if he accelerates some more, but what's for certain is that he doesn't slow down, that maybe the needle on the speedometer is pointing at something like one hundred twenty or one hundred thirty miles per hour, and also that the straight line will at some point stop being straight.

Except that Dwayne Koster is no longer in reality; no, he's in the world of his negative thought, the one that crushed all the others and told him: "You're going to make me silence those frightened horses galloping after you, trampling your brain, insulting your humanity, you're going to make them shut up once and for all." And this time the voice in his head no longer speaks nicely to him at all, suddenly it screams and shouts and just says, Brake! Brake! Brake!

So, as if waking up from a nightmare or something, he looks at his face in the rearview mirror, at his brow, which seemed to stop going pale after a few days. And within a fraction of a second, he's looking at himself as if he had only just gotten there, in his car, as if he had only just left Susan or his university office. He looks straight ahead at the curve taking shape and obviously he slams on the brakes, very hard, brakes that brake really well. Except that it's too late, rather too late, and after that, after that the only sound he hears, even though he keeps braking before he hits the edge of the road, is the wheels spinning in the air, given that it's been a good moment since the sky tilted and he started flying, yes, he's flying through the sky. But he's going to fall back down, it's certain that he's going to fall back down; and that's going to hurt. That's going to hurt really, really badly.

Chapter 9

In the desert, still red in the breaking day, among the mangled metal, despite the blood running down his forehead, Dwayne Koster sees a shadow moving closer to the car and then bending over him. It isn't Milly. It isn't Susan. No, it's Jim Sullivan, who smiles at him and takes him by the hand. And Jim tells him that he can come too, he can come over there, into the desert with him. Over there, far, far away, where there'll be room for him too. So, Dwayne climbs out of the still smoking Dodge and follows Jim among the cacti, far away, over there, where the earth grows hard. And Dwayne walks, he walks over the cracked desert. There you have it. That's America. Dwayne disappears, he disappears into the distance.

SELECTED DALKEY ARCHIVE TITLES

MICHAL AJVAZ, *The Golden Age.*
The Other City.

PIERRE ALBERT-BIROT, *Grabinoulor.*

YUZ ALESHKOVSKY, *Kangaroo.*

FELIPE ALFAU, *Chromos.*
Locos.

JOE AMATO, *Samuel Taylor's Last Night.*

IVAN ÂNGELO, *The Celebration.*
The Tower of Glass.

ANTÓNIO LOBO ANTUNES, *Knowledge of Hell.*
The Splendor of Portugal.

ALAIN ARIAS-MISSON, *Theatre of Incest.*

JOHN ASHBERY & JAMES SCHUYLER, *A Nest of Ninnies.*

ROBERT ASHLEY, *Perfect Lives.*

GABRIELA AVIGUR-ROTEM, *Heatwave and Crazy Birds.*

DJUNA BARNES, *Ladies Almanack.*
Ryder.

JOHN BARTH, *Letters.*
Sabbatical.

DONALD BARTHELME, *The King.*
Paradise.

SVETISLAV BASARA, *Chinese Letter.*

MIQUEL BAUÇÀ, *The Siege in the Room.*

RENÉ BELLETTO, *Dying.*

MAREK BIENCZYK, *Transparency.*

ANDREI BITOV, *Pushkin House.*

ANDREJ BLATNIK, *You Do Understand.*
Law of Desire.

LOUIS PAUL BOON, *Chapel Road.*
My Little War.
Summer in Termuren.

ROGER BOYLAN, *Killoyle.*

IGNÁCIO DE LOYOLA BRANDÃO, *Anonymous Celebrity.*
Zero.

BONNIE BREMSER, *Troia: Mexican Memoirs.*

CHRISTINE BROOKE-ROSE, *Amalgamemnon.*

BRIGID BROPHY, *In Transit.*
The Prancing Novelist.

GERALD L. BRUNS, *Modern Poetry and the Idea of Language.*

GABRIELLE BURTON, *Heartbreak Hotel.*

MICHEL BUTOR, *Degrees.*
Mobile.

G. CABRERA INFANTE, *Infante's Inferno.*
Three Trapped Tigers.

JULIETA CAMPOS, *The Fear of Losing Eurydice.*

ANNE CARSON, *Eros the Bittersweet.*

ORLY CASTEL-BLOOM, *Dolly City.*

LOUIS-FERDINAND CÉLINE, *North.*
Conversations with Professor Y.
London Bridge.

MARIE CHAIX, *The Laurels of Lake Constance.*

HUGO CHARTERIS, *The Tide Is Right.*

ERIC CHEVILLARD, *Demolishing Nisard.*
The Author and Me.

MARC CHOLODENKO, *Mordechai Schamz.*

JOSHUA COHEN, *Witz.*

EMILY HOLMES COLEMAN, *The Shutter of Snow.*

ERIC CHEVILLARD, *The Author and Me.*

ROBERT COOVER, *A Night at the Movies.*

STANLEY CRAWFORD, *Log of the S.S. The Mrs Unguentine.*
Some Instructions to My Wife.

RENÉ CREVEL, *Putting My Foot in It.*

RALPH CUSACK, *Cadenza.*

NICHOLAS DELBANCO, *Sherbrookes.*
The Count of Concord.

NIGEL DENNIS, *Cards of Identity.*

PETER DIMOCK, *A Short Rhetoric for Leaving the Family.*

ARIEL DORFMAN, *Konfidenz.*

COLEMAN DOWELL, *Island People.*
Too Much Flesh and Jabez.

ARKADII DRAGOMOSHCHENKO, *Dust.*

RIKKI DUCORNET, *Phosphor in Dreamland.*
The Complete Butcher's Tales.

FOR A FULL LIST OF PUBLICATIONS, VISIT: www.dalkeyarchive.com

SELECTED DALKEY ARCHIVE TITLES

RIKKI DUCORNET (cont.), *The Jade Cabinet.*
The Fountains of Neptune.

WILLIAM EASTLAKE, *The Bamboo Bed.*
Castle Keep.
Lyric of the Circle Heart.

JEAN ECHENOZ, *Chopin's Move.*

STANLEY ELKIN, *A Bad Man.*
Criers and Kibitzers, Kibitzers and Criers.
The Dick Gibson Show.
The Franchiser.
The Living End.
Mrs. Ted Bliss.

FRANÇOIS EMMANUEL, *Invitation to a Voyage.*

PAUL EMOND, *The Dance of a Sham.*

SALVADOR ESPRIU, *Ariadne in the Grotesque Labyrinth.*

LESLIE A. FIEDLER, *Love and Death in the American Novel.*

JUAN FILLOY, *Op Oloop.*

ANDY FITCH, *Pop Poetics.*

GUSTAVE FLAUBERT, *Bouvard and Pécuchet.*

KASS FLEISHER, *Talking out of School.*

JON FOSSE, *Aliss at the Fire.*
Melancholy.

FORD MADOX FORD, *The March of Literature.*

MAX FRISCH, *I'm Not Stiller.*
Man in the Holocene.

CARLOS FUENTES, *Christopher Unborn.*
Distant Relations.
Terra Nostra.
Where the Air Is Clear.

TAKEHIKO FUKUNAGA, *Flowers of Grass.*

WILLIAM GADDIS, JR., *The Recognitions.*

JANICE GALLOWAY, *Foreign Parts.*
The Trick Is to Keep Breathing.

WILLIAM H. GASS, *Life Sentences.*
The Tunnel.
The World Within the Word.
Willie Masters' Lonesome Wife.

GÉRARD GAVARRY, *Hoppla! 1 2 3.*

ETIENNE GILSON, *The Arts of the Beautiful.*
Forms and Substances in the Arts.

C. S. GISCOMBE, *Giscome Road.*
Here.

DOUGLAS GLOVER, *Bad News of the Heart.*

WITOLD GOMBROWICZ, *A Kind of Testament.*

PAULO EMÍLIO SALES GOMES, *P's Three Women.*

GEORGI GOSPODINOV, *Natural Novel.*

JUAN GOYTISOLO, *Count Julian.*
Juan the Landless.
Makbara.
Marks of Identity.

HENRY GREEN, *Blindness.*
Concluding.
Doting.
Nothing.

JACK GREEN, *Fire the Bastards!*

JIŘÍ GRUŠA, *The Questionnaire.*

MELA HARTWIG, *Am I a Redundant Human Being?*

JOHN HAWKES, *The Passion Artist.*
Whistlejacket.

ELIZABETH HEIGHWAY, ED., *Contemporary Georgian Fiction.*

AIDAN HIGGINS, *Balcony of Europe.*
Blind Man's Bluff.
Bornholm Night-Ferry.
Langrishe, Go Down.
Scenes from a Receding Past.

KEIZO HINO, *Isle of Dreams.*

KAZUSHI HOSAKA, *Plainsong.*

ALDOUS HUXLEY, *Antic Hay.*
Point Counter Point.
Those Barren Leaves.
Time Must Have a Stop.

NAOYUKI II, *The Shadow of a Blue Cat.*

DRAGO JANČAR, *The Tree with No Name.*

MIKHEIL JAVAKHISHVILI, *Kvachi.*

GERT JONKE, *The Distant Sound.*
Homage to Czerny.
The System of Vienna.

SELECTED DALKEY ARCHIVE TITLES

NICHOLAS MOSLEY, *Accident.*
Assassins.
Catastrophe Practice.
A Garden of Trees.
Hopeful Monsters.
Imago Bird.
Inventing God.
Look at the Dark.
Metamorphosis.
Natalie Natalia.
Serpent.

WARREN MOTTE, *Fables of the Novel: French Fiction since 1990.*
Fiction Now: The French Novel in the 21st Century.
Mirror Gazing.
Oulipo: A Primer of Potential Literature.

GERALD MURNANE, *Barley Patch.*
Inland.

YVES NAVARRE, *Our Share of Time.*
Sweet Tooth.

DOROTHY NELSON, *In Night's City.*
Tar and Feathers.

ESHKOL NEVO, *Homesick.*

WILFRIDO D. NOLLEDO, *But for the Lovers.*

BORIS A. NOVAK, *The Master of Insomnia.*

FLANN O'BRIEN, *At Swim-Two-Birds.*
The Best of Myles.
The Dalkey Archive.
The Hard Life.
The Poor Mouth.
The Third Policeman.

CLAUDE OLLIER, *The Mise-en-Scène.*
Wert and the Life Without End.

PATRIK OUŘEDNÍK, *Europeana.*
The Opportune Moment, 1855.

BORIS PAHOR, *Necropolis.*

FERNANDO DEL PASO, *News from the Empire.*
Palinuro of Mexico.

ROBERT PINGET, *The Inquisitory.*
Mahu or The Material.
Trio.

MANUEL PUIG, *Betrayed by Rita Hayworth.*
The Buenos Aires Affair.
Heartbreak Tango.

RAYMOND QUENEAU, *The Last Days.*
Odile.
Pierrot Mon Ami.
Saint Glinglin.

ANN QUIN, *Berg.*
Passages.
Three.
Tripticks.

ISHMAEL REED, *The Free-Lance Pallbearers.*
The Last Days of Louisiana Red.
Ishmael Reed: The Plays.
Juice!
The Terrible Threes.
The Terrible Twos.
Yellow Back Radio Broke-Down.

JASIA REICHARDT, *15 Journeys Warsaw to London.*

JOÃO UBALDO RIBEIRO, *House of the Fortunate Buddhas.*

JEAN RICARDOU, *Place Names.*

RAINER MARIA RILKE, *The Notebooks of Malte Laurids Brigge.*

JULIÁN RÍOS, *The House of Ulysses.*
Larva: A Midsummer Night's Babel.
Poundemonium.

ALAIN ROBBE-GRILLET, *Project for a Revolution in New York.*
A Sentimental Novel.

AUGUSTO ROA BASTOS, *I the Supreme.*

DANIËL ROBBERECHTS, *Arriving in Avignon.*

JEAN ROLIN, *The Explosion of the Radiator Hose.*

OLIVIER ROLIN, *Hotel Crystal.*

ALIX CLEO ROUBAUD, *Alix's Journal.*

JACQUES ROUBAUD, *The Form of a City Changes Faster, Alas, Than the Human Heart.*
The Great Fire of London.
Hortense in Exile.
Hortense Is Abducted.
Mathematics: The Plurality of Worlds of Lewis.
Some Thing Black.

SELECTED DALKEY ARCHIVE TITLES

RAYMOND ROUSSEL, *Impressions of Africa.*

VEDRANA RUDAN, *Night.*

PABLO M. RUIZ, *Four Cold Chapters on the Possibility of Literature.*

GERMAN SADULAEV, *The Maya Pill.*

TOMAŽ ŠALAMUN, *Soy Realidad.*

LYDIE SALVAYRE, *The Company of Ghosts.*
The Lecture.
The Power of Flies.

LUIS RAFAEL SÁNCHEZ, *Macho Camacho's Beat.*

SEVERO SARDUY, *Cobra & Maitreya.*

NATHALIE SARRAUTE, *Do You Hear Them?*
Martereau.
The Planetarium.

STIG SÆTERBAKKEN, *Siamese.*
Self-Control.
Through the Night.

ARNO SCHMIDT, *Collected Novellas.*
Collected Stories.
Nobodaddy's Children.
Two Novels.

ASAF SCHURR, *Motti.*

GAIL SCOTT, *My Paris.*

DAMION SEARLS, *What We Were Doing and Where We Were Going.*

JUNE AKERS SEESE, *Is This What Other Women Feel Too?*

BERNARD SHARE, *Inish.*
Transit.

VIKTOR SHKLOVSKY, *Bowstring.*
Literature and Cinematography.
Theory of Prose.
Third Factory.
Zoo, or Letters Not about Love.

PIERRE SINIAC, *The Collaborators.*

KJERSTI A. SKOMSVOLD, *The Faster I Walk, the Smaller I Am.*

JOSEF ŠKVORECKÝ, *The Engineer of Human Souls.*

GILBERT SORRENTINO, *Aberration of Starlight.*
Blue Pastoral.
Crystal Vision.
Imaginative Qualities of Actual Things.
Mulligan Stew. Red the Fiend.
Steelwork.
Under the Shadow.

MARKO SOSIČ, *Ballerina, Ballerina.*

ANDRZEJ STASIUK, *Dukla.*
Fado.

GERTRUDE STEIN, *The Making of Americans.*
A Novel of Thank You.

LARS SVENDSEN, *A Philosophy of Evil.*

PIOTR SZEWC, *Annihilation.*

GONÇALO M. TAVARES, *A Man: Klaus Klump.*
Jerusalem.
Learning to Pray in the Age of Technique.

LUCIAN DAN TEODOROVICI, *Our Circus Presents . . .*

NIKANOR TERATOLOGEN, *Assisted Living.*

STEFAN THEMERSON, *Hobson's Island.*
The Mystery of the Sardine.
Tom Harris.

TAEKO TOMIOKA, *Building Waves.*

JOHN TOOMEY, *Sleepwalker.*

DUMITRU TSEPENEAG, *Hotel Europa.*
The Necessary Marriage.
Pigeon Post.
Vain Art of the Fugue.

ESTHER TUSQUETS, *Stranded.*

DUBRAVKA UGRESIC, *Lend Me Your Character.*
Thank You for Not Reading.

TOR ULVEN, *Replacement.*

MATI UNT, *Brecht at Night.*
Diary of a Blood Donor.
Things in the Night.

ÁLVARO URIBE & OLIVIA SEARS, EDS., *Best of Contemporary Mexican Fiction.*

ELOY URROZ, *Friction.*
The Obstacles.

LUISA VALENZUELA, *Dark Desires and the Others.*
He Who Searches.

PAUL VERHAEGHEN, *Omega Minor.*

BORIS VIAN, *Heartsnatcher.*

FOR A FULL LIST OF PUBLICATIONS, VISIT: www.dalkeyarchive.com

SELECTED DALKEY ARCHIVE TITLES

LLORENÇ VILLALONGA, *The Dolls' Room.*

TOOMAS VINT, *An Unending Landscape.*

ORNELA VORPSI, *The Country Where No One Ever Dies.*

AUSTRYN WAINHOUSE, *Hedyphagetica.*

CURTIS WHITE, *America's Magic Mountain.*
The Idea of Home.
Memories of My Father Watching TV.
Requiem.

DIANE WILLIAMS,
Excitability: Selected Stories.
Romancer Erector.

DOUGLAS WOOLF, *Wall to Wall.*
Ya! & John-Juan.

JAY WRIGHT, *Polynomials and Pollen.*
The Presentable Art of Reading Absence.

PHILIP WYLIE, *Generation of Vipers.*

MARGUERITE YOUNG, *Angel in the Forest.*
Miss MacIntosh, My Darling.

REYOUNG, *Unbabbling.*

VLADO ŽABOT, *The Succubus.*

ZORAN ŽIVKOVIĆ , *Hidden Camera.*

LOUIS ZUKOFSKY, *Collected Fiction.*

VITOMIL ZUPAN, *Minuet for Guitar.*

SCOTT ZWIREN, *God Head.*

AND MORE . . .